For once
Francesca was adamant

She could see that he was very ill. "I'm not going to argue with you, Oliver," she said. "Neither am I going to leave this house until you're well enough to be left alone."

"All right," he agreed weakly, "you win this time around. Although what the hell you think you're trying to prove by playing the ministering angel—"

Francesca flinched beneath the contempt in his voice. "I'm not trying to prove anything," she told him quietly.

"That's just as well, because as I've already told you, there's no place for an innocent like you in my life, Francesca."

"I agree," she said proudly. "And even if there was, I doubt very much that I would want to be in it."

Instinctively then, she stepped back from the fierce anger that flared up in his eyes.

FRANCES RODING is a new name in the Harlequin romance series. However, we feel sure that the writing style of this British-based author will soon make her popular with romance readers everywhere.

Books by Frances Roding

HARLEQUIN PRESENTS
1052—OPEN TO INFLUENCE
1163—MAN OF STONE
1190—A DIFFERENT DREAM

HARLEQUIN ROMANCE
2901—SOME SORT OF SPELL

FRANCES RODING

a law unto himself

Harlequin Books

TORONTO • NEW YORK • LONDON
AMSTERDAM • PARIS • SYDNEY • HAMBURG
STOCKHOLM • ATHENS • TOKYO • MILAN

Harlequin Presents first edition October 1989
ISBN 0-373-11213-0

Original hardcover edition published in 1989
by Mills & Boon Limited

Printed in U.S.A.

CHAPTER ONE

As THE Alitalia plane circled the city of her birth, Francesca looked down on it with a faint frown of mingled bewilderment and pain that touched the heart of the stewardess walking down the aisle, and prompted her to comment to her co-workers that it was disconcerting to see such a look of vulnerable loneliness on such a beautiful woman's face.

'Who are you talking about?' the chief stewardess asked her.

'The woman four rows from the front, with the beautiful cashmere separates and the long dark hair.'

'Ah, yes... Francesca di Valeria.'

'You know her?' the more junior stewardess enquired.

'Not personally.' She gave a wry smile. 'She's way out of my social league, but I know *of* her. She comes from a family of very wealthy industrialists. She was due to marry the son of an equally powerful and wealthy family this summer, but the wedding had to be called off at the last moment because the groom had secretly married someone else. There was quite a lot in the papers about it at the time.' She gave a cynical shrug. 'Her family were well compensated for their embarrassment. A large contract from the family of the ex-bridegroom. And it was an arranged match, anyway. Everyone knows that.'

If Francesca had been able to overhear her comments, they wouldn't have surprised her. In the close-knit, gossipy world of the Italian aristocracy, it was common knowledge that their two families had decided that she and Paolo would eventually marry while they themselves were in their cradles. The marriage hadn't even been by her parents' choice but by her grandfather's, the powerful, autocratic and extremely domineering Duca di Valeria, and Francesca had grown up knowing that one day she would be Paolo's wife.

She had not been in love with him, it was true, but she had grown so used to the idea of eventually being his wife that the shock of discovering that he had deserted her, practically at the altar, for someone else had thrown her into complete disruption.

Her whole life...her education...everything had been geared towards her becoming Paolo's wife, towards the fact that one day she would take over from Paolo's mother, the present Marchesa, as the matriarch of the family—a family with vast interests in commerce and industry; a family with a history that spanned many generations; a proud, upright, formidable family, much like her own.

Now all that was gone.

Paolo's sisters and cousins avoided her if they saw her in the street. Their mutual friends made embarrassed murmurs of sympathy; even her own grandfather sometimes looked at her with an irate pity that said more than any words that he blamed her in part for Paolo's defection.

And it was because of this...this almost total severing of her life with a blow that left her unable to go back to what had once been, and yet with no clear idea in her mind of her way forward, that she was leaving her home.

She had a university education and a good brain. Gone were the days when Italian daughters were kept cosseted and protected from the world.

She had even worked for a while, albeit for her godfather, but there had been a tacit understanding that this leniency—this delay in her marriage to Paolo—was a tactful means of allowing *him* time to mature and come to realise what an asset she would be as his wife.

Such marriages were not uncommon among the families that formed the social circle in which her family moved. Marriage was, after all, a serious business, involving not only the young couple concerned but also their parents, grandparents, aunts, uncles and cousins.

The hardest thing of all to bear had been the silences that seemed to fall whenever she walked into a room...the way people watched her, discussed her, pitied her...for who would marry her now? She who had been destined almost from birth for such a high position.

She had endured it for as long as she could, through a mixture of pride and concern for her parents.

Her grandfather had never approved of his eldest son's choice of bride, the pretty English girl who had come to Italy to care for the twin nieces of his cousin, but her father had insisted on marrying her and they had been very, very happy.

The birth of three sons, followed by a daughter, had gone a long way to softening the Duca's at-

titude, but now, with Paolo's rejection of
Francesca, all the old bitterness had flared up, and
her grandfather, whose fiery temper was notorious,
had almost gone as far as to suggest that it was
because of Francesca's English blood that Paolo
had left her for someone else.

That had been when Francesca had decided she
had had enough, and it was through the good of-
fices of her godparents that she was now bound for
the country of her mother's birth, to spend an ex-
tended visit with Elliott and Beatrice Chalmers, a
couple whom Francesca had often heard her godparents mention but whom she had never met.

The English couple had two children, a little boy
of three and a baby of six months. They lived in
the country, Francesca had been told, and her god-
mother had remarked solicitously that she hoped
the fresh English air would bring the colour back
to her pale face, and the kilos to her slender body.

In her mother's eyes, Francesca had read her
relief in seeing her daughter make the first decision
since the catastrophe of the telegram's arrival on
the morning of her wedding, announcing that there
would be no bridegroom. Normally positive by
nature, Francesca had sunk into a swamp of apathy,
retreating inside herself as the only means she had,
in a large and very voluble Italian family, of finding
a retreat where she could gather up her strength
and lick her wounds.

And there *were* wounds. She had not loved Paolo
in the way that romantic novels described the
emotion, it was true, but she *had* cared for him,
respected him . . . and looked forward to being his
wife and the mother of his children and to the life

they would live together. She had thought he looked forward to them too, so it had been a cruel blow to discover not only that he had deserted her for someone else, but also that he had not had the courage to inform her of his decision himself.

What was almost as hard to endure was the realisation that there had been friends who had known what was going on, but who had said nothing. Her trust had been shattered and left in a million splintered pieces. Not just her trust in others, but her trust in herself as well, and she now looked into the past with revulsion, seeing herself as stupidly self-satisfied, so absorbed in her own contentment that she had been blind to reality; so unaware of the feelings of others that she had never even guessed that something was wrong; so caught up in the pleasant meandering of her own life that it never even occurred to her that someone else might yearn for the swift, heady rush of the youthful torrent.

What was *wrong* with her, that she had never felt any need to experience what Paolo must have experienced? Falling in love, being in love; to her these had been foolish pastimes, suitable only for teenagers; dangerous waters through which she had happily passed unscathed to reach these maturely reflective years of her mid-twenties. Not even as a teenager had she wanted to fall in love, seeing it as a risky, impractical experience, and at twenty-four to Paolo's twenty-five, the idea that he might fall in love, had anyone put it to her, would have struck her as too ludicrous to even merit a reply.

Now she knew better. Now she knew herself better as well, since she had used the months since the wedding as a period of intense inner reflection and analysis, and she had come to see, in her quiet determination to concentrate all her skills and intelligence in fulfilling her role as Paolo's wife, a deeply buried desire to atone to her grandfather for her father's rebellion, and her mother's English blood.

That realisation had made her feel deeply ashamed, because her parents loved her dearly, cherished her deeply, and cared far, far more for her than did her arrogant grandfather, to whom a granddaughter could never have the importance of a grandson.

Her parents had seen her off at the airport, her mother whispering fiercely that she was glad she had not married Paolo.

'He was never good enough for you, my darling,' she had told her. 'I want you to know the same kind of love I've shared with your father. And you will know it.'

Would she? Francesca grimaced wryly to herself, a soft twist of full lips painted in the autumn's latest fashion colour.

Somehow she doubted it... For one thing, she didn't particularly want to. If these last few months had taught her one thing about herself, they had taught her the value of being independent.

Her university degree, her knowledge of the history of her country and its dynasties, her very genuine love of searching out elusive facts had, according to her godfather, given her an invaluable foundation on which to build a new kind of life...a career to fulfil her instead of marriage...the exciting challenge of the real world, instead of the enclosed atmosphere of a protective Italian family.

He had helped her to get started, had encouraged and praised her, had given her work to do, and she had found that she thrived on the challenge.

Even so, there was still a vast emptiness in her life...a feeling of alienation...a desire to escape, which she had finally and reluctantly given in to by accepting Beatrice Chalmers' kind invitation to stay with them.

'Do you think she'll be comfortable here, Elliott? She's been used to so much more luxurious surroundings,' Beatrice fretted as she studied her pretty guest suite with an anxious frown.

'From what Carlo told us about her, I doubt she'll be very concerned with her surroundings,' Elliott told her drily. 'I hope to God she isn't going to be constantly awash with tears and laments.'

'Oh, Elliott, that isn't fair,' Beatrice reproached him. 'Lucia said she had dealt with the whole thing very bravely. It can't have been easy. You won't forget to pick her up from the airport, will you?'

'Would I dare?' Elliott asked drily.

'Oh, and that reminds me...I've asked Oliver over for dinner on Friday,' Beatrice interrupted him briefly.

'Bea,' Elliott warned her. 'I hope you aren't thinking of matchmaking...'

He saw his wife's guilty flush and sighed, reaching out to tousle her glossy dark hair.

'I suppose there's no point in my telling you that you're playing with fire, is there?'

'Because Oliver's a misogynist?' she responded spiritedly.

'Oliver's been badly burned, Bea,' he told her gently. 'And because of it he's inclined to let the world know that he's now fireproof. He won't take kindly to being manipulated into providing a bit of light relief for our lamenting Lucretia, you know.'

He saw how her face had fallen and kissed her lightly. Four years of marriage, and she still had the power to move him in a way that no one else could ever match.

'I must go,' he whispered against her hair. 'I've got a board meeting at ten.'

Watching him drive away, Beatrice wondered if she should perhaps cancel Friday's dinner party. Guiltily she acknowledged that it was true that she had deliberately invited Oliver hoping that the presence of a single, attractive male might help to raise Francesca's spirits a little; especially such a fascinating male as Oliver. And he *was* fascinating, with those distinctive silver, all-seeing eyes and that shock of thick, dark hair so at odds with the curious lightness of his eyes. He could be charming too when he chose, although he invariably directed his light-hearted flirtatious remarks to women he knew full well were perfectly happy with their existing partners, and women who, moreover, had the social skills to return the volleyed flattery with easy sophistication. It was also true that he often chose to exhibit these skills in front of some poor unfortunate who had made it all too plain that she was dangerously on the verge of falling heavily for him. He had a way of nipping such affections in the bud that was brutal and very, very effective. Beatrice gave a faint shiver. Perhaps she had not been so clever after all, but because she had invited several other couples for dinner as well, wanting to introduce Francesca to as many new people as possible, she had decided that Oliver was hardly likely to suspect her of matchmaking.

Not that she was doing, really... although she had to admit there was a definite temptation. How old was he now? Thirty-something... four or five most likely; and it was eight years since Kristie had left him in such a spectacular blaze of publicity, claiming that their daughter was not his after all and that she was going to America to join her lover and Katie's father.

Other people endured similar tragedies. But other men were not Oliver, Beatrice admitted to herself.

That steely pride of his would not have taken kindly to the gleeful publicity of the gutter Press at the downfall of his marriage. Not since he had made it plain how little time he had for them when his first book had been such a huge success.

They had even speculated that losing his wife and child might make him lose the ability to write, but that had not proved the case, and Oliver had gone from strength to strength, his powerfully evocative novels with their accurate historical backgrounds and their vivid challenging characters had remained at the top of the best-seller lists throughout the world.

His new book was set in both England and Italy, a complicated family saga spanning several generations and involving a wealth of internecine treachery of the type for which his books were justly famous.

And it was here that Beatrice had a tiny stab of guilt, because she had not told Elliott exactly what it was she had in mind.

All that was needed now was for both parties to be tactfully approached with the idea, and she was hoping that the dinner party on Friday would provide an ideal means of breaking the ice. She intended to say nothing to Francesca about Oliver, but planned to draw the girl out over the dinner-table, hoping to arouse Oliver's interest. It struck her now that she might have been rather over-ambitious, but she was reluctant to abandon a plan that showed such potential promise, and so she crossed her fingers childishly and promised herself that all would go well, and that she wasn't match-making at all . . . rather, what she was doing was a form of head-hunting, albeit of an extremely freelance variety.

She would be met at Heathrow, Francesca had been told, but in the busy sea of faces in the Arrivals lounge it was impossible to pick out anyone holding up a card bearing her name, so the sudden shock of someone taking hold of her arm made her tense and spin round.

'Sorry, I didn't mean to startle you. I'm Elliott Chalmers, and I think you're Francesca, aren't you?'

Francesca focused on him: a tall, blunt-faced man with a commanding air of authority, and a faintly wry smile.

He made her feel rather like a foolish schoolgirl as he escorted her across the concourse, collected her luggage, and marshalled her outside to where his car was waiting, but at least his blunt, no-nonsense attitude was preferable to the kind of heavy gallantry, not unmixed with sexual speculation, she had been subjected to increasingly of late, and which she found both irritating and distasteful, and from the most surprising of sources.

Here was a man one could trust even if one could not always agree with him, she decided shrewdly. He was also a man who would respect one's rights to one's own opinions, even if he did attempt to steam-roller them.

At home it had been mild and sunny; here in London it was damp and cold. Francesca shivered in her thin wool suit, wishing she had worn the heavier top coat that was packed away in her cases... New cases, because the only ones she possessed were those which had been ordered for her honeymoon, and stamped by Vuitton with her married initials. She winced a little, and hoped that her gesture would be mistakenly put down to the cold.

Her new suitcases bore no initials, but they had come from Gucci and had been very expensive. Her father had insisted on buying them for her. Like all Italian men, he adored spoiling his womenfolk. The new Valentino wardrobe inside the cases had been another parental gift.

Francesca had worn designer clothes almost from her teens. Her family was wealthy and in Italy good dressing was important, but this was the first time she had worn Valentino. He was considered a little fast by Paolo's mother, and so Francesca had subdued her own desire to experiment with his innovative styles and strong colours and had instead

settled for the designer favoured by her mother-in-
law to be.

Now she did not have to weigh such consider-
ations any longer; she was free to do exactly as she
wished. It was an extremely novel realisation, and
she was only just beginning to learn not to be
frightened of it; like a crab without its protective
shell, she had to subdue the urge to scuttle away
and hide herself because she felt so vulnerable.

'Mm . . . I wonder if we'll get all this lot in the
car.'

She looked at Elliott and saw to her relief that
he was teasing her. She responded with a smile, her
first proper smile in a very long time, she realised,
her face muscles feeling slightly stiff.

The dark blue Jaguar was a new model, polished
and shiny, but inside, on the back seat where Elliott
had suggested she might prefer to sit for comfort,
were a couple of books of nursery rhymes and some
children's toys.

'You have a son and a daughter, I believe,' she
commented quietly once they had cleared the heavy
traffic of the airport approaches.

'Yes, Dominic and Rebecca. That's why I'm
meeting you, and not Bea. Henrietta, the mainstay
of our household, is away having a few days holiday
at the moment, but she will be back at the weekend.
I take it that Lucia has filled you in with details of
the Bellaire and Chalmers families?'

'Yes. Your father married Beatrice's mother, but
she had been previously married to a fellow actor,
Charles Bellaire, and after your father's death and
Charles's subsequent divorce, they remarried . . .'

'Yes, and went on to have four more children: the twins, Sebastian and Benedict, Miranda and last, but definitely not least, William. I dare say you will meet them all in due course, although probably not Lucilla, who is both mine and Beatrice's half-sister. She's the only child of my father's marriage to Beatrice's mother. She's in the States at the moment with her husband, Nick Barrington. He has extensive interests and connections in Hollywood, and they've gone there to recruit a new star for a new film that is presently casting.'

Francesca had heard all about her hostess's fascinating family background, so very different from her own with its staid ranks of *ducas* and *contes*; its many, many Valerian aunts and uncles; its traditions and its shibboleths.

'Bad flight?' Elliott asked her, glancing into his driving mirror and observing her too pale face.

She was a beautiful woman, even with the sculptured pared-down thinness of her face. Her hair was like polished silk, hanging thick and heavy on to her shoulders, her make-up immaculate, the golden eyes wary and shuttered, and yet for all her poise and beauty, for all the immaculateness of her appearance, there was none of the plastic dullness that sometimes characterised such perfection.

Her elegance was unmistakably Italian, and yet there was at the same time just a hint of her English heritage, in the mobility of her face and that faint, betraying wariness of her eyes.

He would have to warn Bea again not to expose Francesca to Oliver. He would make mincemeat out

of her, and the girl was just vulnerable enough to
be hurt by his abrasiveness.

He could see Oliver's viewpoint, though; a man
who had been deceived in the way that he had been
deceived was bound to have been hardened by the
experience and to want to hold the female sex at a
distance.

The prettiness of the English countryside, even in
the gloom of the damp October afternoon, was a
surprise to Francesca. Her mother had come from
the north, a small mining community to which she
had no desire to return and with which she had no
ties, since she had been orphaned young.

But this...this soft mingling of greens and golds,
this pale sunlight that softened cream stone walls
ancient with lichen...this very quiet delicacy of
colour appealed strongly to her. Even the autumn
melancholy of the landscape was in tune with her
own sombre thoughts; not of the man she had lost,
because she was honest enough to admit to herself
that she had not loved him; not even for the
honours that would have been hers as his wife.
No...it was the loss of self she mourned most...the
realisation that she had blindly and willingly
allowed herself to be formed into the most suitable
image for a granddaughter of the Duca di Valeria.
She had even connived at the image-making herself,
had willing allowed herself to be moulded and
fashioned into an artificial role. It was the betrayal
of herself that hurt the most; the realisation that
through both laziness and cowardice she had abandoned her rights to be herself...to be independent
and to make her own life.

Once while she was at university there had been a boy. He had wanted to be her lover... a wild *ragazzo* from the streets of Naples, sponsored by a wealthy benefactor because of his intelligence. She had not been able to hide from him her indifference to his feelings.

He had accused her then of not being 'real', of not being a person in her own right. She had listened gravely to his insults and then calmly cut him out of her life, relieved, if the truth was known, to end the acquaintanceship with him, because deep down inside her part of her had been disturbed by him, not sexually, but mentally, and she had resented that quiet ripple across the placid surface of her life.

How complacent she had been. How stupidly, wantonly complacent.

She closed her eyes, and Elliott, glancing at her through his mirror, was thankful that they were nearly home. If she was going to burst into tears, he would rather it was when Bea was there to cope and commiserate. As the thought formed, her eyelids lifted, and the golden eyes flashed proud rejection of his thoughts back at him.

So she was not as remote and serene as she appeared. She had pride and spirit. She would need them if she was to succeed in her plans to form a completely new life for herself, more in step with the modern world than the old-fashioned protected one of her grandfather.

'Nearly there,' he told her, turning off the main road and driving through the small Cotswold village that was only a handful of miles from his and Beatrice's home.

The village delighted Francesca, and she swiftly recognised the Tudor architecture of the stone cottages. History was her love, and because her mother was English she had studied British history in almost as much detail as she had Italian.

'Here we are.'

Elliott turned in through the gates of the mellow Cotswold house. Even before they had left the car, the front door was thrown open and a young woman came hurrying out. Older than Francesca, she nevertheless had an unexpected youthfulness that the Italian girl hadn't anticipated, having heard many times of how Beatrice had been the mainstay and substitute mother to her family after her parents' death.

She wasn't as tall as Francesca herself, and was slightly plumper, a baby clutched in one arm while a blond-haired little boy ran forward to fling himself into Elliott's arms almost before the car door was open.

'Welcome to England,' Beatrice greeted her with a warm smile. 'Come inside. You must be feeling the cold after Italy. You must tell me if your room isn't warm enough. The central heating's on, but all the bedrooms have fires and we can light one for you if necessary. I hope you won't mind dining *en famille* tonight. Henrietta, who runs the house and us, is away visiting friends at the moment, and I'm afraid everything is rather disorganised.

'By the way,' Beatrice asked her, as she urged her inside the house, 'what are we to call you? Francesca . . . or do you have a nickname—Chessie perhaps?'

Beatrice's warm, friendly smile touched something inside her that reminded her very much of her mother.

No one in *il Duca*'s household was allowed the informality of having their name abbreviated, and consequently all her life she had been Francesca; a graceful, elegant name, which she suddenly realised had often been a very difficult one to live up to. Chessie, now ... Chessie conjured up a very different image indeed. A Chessie might be permitted all kinds of follies and foolishnesses never permitted a Francesca, and so, turning her back on the rigorous training of twenty-four years, Francesca returned Beatrice's smile and said firmly, 'Chessie will be fine.'

Chessie ...

She savoured the name to herself as she followed Beatrice upstairs. It had an untrammelled, freedom-loving sound to it that she liked; it made her feel young and vibrant ... it made her feel she was free of the burden of being the granddaughter of the Duca di Valeria, the rejected promised wife of Paolo di Calveri.

From her room she could see over the surrounding countryside. She felt curiously at home here in a way she had not expected. She liked her hostess, and suspected she would also like her host once she had got to know him.

Initially she had protested when her godparents had arranged this break for her, but she had been too listless to resist their plans. Now that she was here, though, she wondered that she had never thought of coming before. Here no one knew about her and Paolo, apart from her hosts. No one cared that she was the granddaughter of *il duca*...no one would ever call her 'Francesca' in that curt, disapproving tone of her grandfather's that had so often chilled the warmth of her youth.

Here she was Chessie...a young woman just like any other, with enough qualifications to find herself a job should she so wish...with surely her whole future spread out in front of her, rather like her view of the pretty countryside.

A sense of eagerness and adventure she had not experienced in a long long time flowed through her. She started to unpack her cases, humming as she did so.

CHAPTER TWO

'THIS dinner party, are you sure you do not need any help?' Francesca asked gravely, with memories of her mother's dinner parties and the days of anxiety and tension that preceded them lest she fell short of her father-in-law's exalted standards in some way and called down his wrath upon her head.

Beatrice laughed.

'No...everything's under control. Most of the food was prepared last week before Henry left, and it's in the freezer...as for the rest...well, our friends are very easygoing and quite happy to take pot luck.'

'Pot luck?' Francesca wrinkled her forehead and obligingly Beatrice explained the phrase for her.

'But the silver—the crystal... You have no maid, and surely these will need to be cleaned?'

'Henry and I did all that before she left. We live quite simply here, Chessie,' Beatrice told her gently.

Immediately Francesca flushed, and Beatrice was quick to comfort her.

'Please don't be embarrassed. We know that you come from a very different and far grander background than ours.'

'My mother says that the formality insisted upon by my grandfather is no longer necessary, but nothing anyone can say will make him change his ways. My mother says he takes pride in them. He is very arrogant.'

'And you both love him and resent him,' Beatrice guessed. 'It's hard, isn't it, to constantly strive for the approval and affection of someone who only seems to notice you're there when you do the wrong things?'

'Very,' Francesca agreed bleakly. 'So...if I cannot help with the meal, perhaps I could take charge of the children.'

'No. What you *can* do is to make yourself so alluringly beautiful that none of my male guests will be able to take their eyes off you, and with their wives watching them watching you, I shan't have to worry if my food isn't up to scratch, shall I?' Beatrice teased her, calmly accepting the change of subject and its implications. She had no intentions of putting any pressure on Francesca to discuss the past or her family with her; she simply wanted the Italian girl to feel at home with them. Sometimes she had such a look of taut constraint that Beatrice ached to tell her that what she was enduring would eventually pass, but she sensed that Francesca was too proud to welcome any intrusion into her personal pain, however well-meant.

'Could you help us?' Lucia had begged her in that unexpected telephone call four weeks ago. 'We have a god-daughter, a charming, beautiful girl, who is simply fading away before our eyes. She needs a change of scene, a change of life-style...'' And she had gone on to explain to Beatrice exactly what had happened.

'It is not in her heart that she is hurt, but in her pride, in her belief in herself, and these can be even harder wounds to bear. But I think they will heal more easily if she is away from Italy, and more especially if she is away from her grandfather.'

And so Beatrice had readily agreed to invite Francesca to stay. And not just because of the debt she herself owed the Fioris.

It had been Lucia who had counselled her so wisely when she had thought her own love for Elliott to be hopeless—she had believed that it must be impossible for him to love her. But even without that debt she would still have wanted to help.

Elliott arrived home an hour before their dinner guests were due.

'I take it Oliver's still included in the guest list?' he asked her, after mixing them both a drink, bringing them up to the bedroom, and telling her to sit down for five minutes and relax.

'Yes.' She looked at him uncertainly. 'Elliott, I'm not trying to matchmake, but it occurred to me that Chessie might be the ideal solution to Oliver's research problem. You know he's desperate to find someone to take over the Italian research on his latest book, and that he can't get away himself. Chessie has a history degree.'

'She also has a stunning figure, a beautiful face, and the kind of vulnerability that will make Oliver tear her to shreds if he gets the mood on him, and you and I both know it,' Elliott warned her grimly, interrupting her, and then adding, 'I'm not saying it isn't a good idea . . . on the face of it. But Oliver's lethal. He's also a man and very human . . .'

'Meaning?' Beatrice questioned him uncertainly.

'Meaning that to you, my dear wife, he may behave like a perfect gentleman, but where women less wrapped up in their husbands are concerned, he can be...well, let's just say that he has all the usual male appetites and that he's quite capable of satisfying them and then ejecting the woman concerned from his life with rather brutal efficiency.'

'You think he'd try to seduce Chessie?' Beatrice asked uneasily.

'I don't know. He's one of those men who's a law unto himself, and I wouldn't like to predict what he might do.'

Beatrice's eyes rounded in astonishment. Her husband was an astute judge of character and normally very crisp and to the point in giving his opinion of his fellow men.

'Well, I only thought that tonight we could see how they get on, and then...'

'Liar,' Elliott interrupted her ruthlessly. 'You intended to dangle Chessie in front of him like a very tempting piece of bait, in the hope that her expertise in Italian history will prove so irresistible that it will outweigh his legendary dislike of working with women.'

'And do you think it will?' Beatrice asked him slyly.

Elliott looked at her in their bedroom mirror and eventually said grimly, 'Unfortunately, yes.'

'Unfortunately for Oliver or for Chessie?'

'Potentially, for them both!'

In her own bedroom, Chessie too was looking into a mirror, but she was alone with her reflection, unlike Beatrice and Elliott.

'Nothing too formal,' Beatrice had advised her when she had asked her what she should wear, and she only hoped that what she had chosen would be suitable.

Her grandfather had set great store by the correct appearance, and Chessie was not sure where on the scale of formality her scarlet Valentino wool crêpe dress would stand.

True, it was very plain, the soft fabric draped subtly to reveal her curves...true it had a high, round neck, and long, all-covering sleeves...but it was also short, just above the knee, and the colour itself was so eye-catching that it scarcely needed any further adornment.

She had left her hair down, catching it back with a gilt bow. She was wearing matching gold bow earrings from which a pearl was suspended, and a collection of fine gold bangles which made a soft musical sound when she moved.

Sheer black tights, high-heeled suede pumps, the Chamade perfume she had switched to only months ago, and which she still wasn't completely sure about. It was so different from the cool, fresh fragrance she had worn before. A fragrance chosen by her grandfather as being 'suitable' for a young woman of his house.

The dining-room of the Cotswold house was barely a fifth of the size of that in her grandfather's *palazzo* but it had a welcoming warmth that Francesca infinitely preferred.

The problem was, as one of her aunts had austerely told her, when as a teenager she had dared to complain that the vast, echoing rooms of the seventeenth-century *palazzo* had no warmth about them, that she and her mother had been ridiculously indulged by her father, who had broken the tradition of centuries in refusing to move his new bride into the family home, but who had instead bought a pretty little villa on the outskirts of the city with its own private garden and an informal courtyard that Francesca remembered with nostalgic longing.

When her grandfather's health had started to fail, though, her father had given in to family pressure to move himself and his family into the family home.

The *palazzo* was a vast, echoing place with marble floors, and a quantity of rococo gilt mirrors. It cost a fortune to maintain, and it was only by judicious marriages and deploying their resources into commerce that the family had been able to retain a home that was really more a museum-piece than suitable for modern-day living.

Francesca knew that her mother had never felt wholly comfortable living there. For one thing, she was no longer really in charge of her own household, the *palazzo* being run by a maiden aunt of the family, who refused to allow anyone to take over from her.

The *palazzo* possessed a vast warren of higgledy-piggledy rooms on the floors above the grand reception-rooms, more than enough to house all the aunts, uncles, and cousins who lived there.

It must be rather nice to be like Beatrice and to have to share this lovely home with only one's husband and children. Had *she* married Paolo, her home would have been in a *palazzo* even more enormous than her grandfather's. Francesca frowned thoughtfully. If she had never really looked forward to such a prospect, then why had she not said so? Why had she allowed her grandfather to dominate her life?

'Do you think everything looks all right?' Beatrice asked her, anxiously coming into the room and mistaking her frowning introspection for a critical study of her table.

'It looks lovely,' Francesca told her truthfully. 'What time do your guests arrive?'

'Any minute now. Elliott will serve them drinks in the drawing-room, while I help Henry in the kitchen. I wonder, Chessie, would you be very kind and help Elliott to entertain them? I've invited two other couples: the local doctor and her husband, who's a lecturer at Oxford; a business colleague of Elliott's who lives a few miles away and his wife; and another neighbour of ours, Oliver Newton. He's a writer. I don't know if you've heard of him. He writes under the name of Dominic Lacey.'

'I've seen his books. He writes thrillers, doesn't he?'

'Sort of. He's an expert on Elizabethan England, and he sets his books in that period. They're very popular. He's having problems with his latest one, though. His main character, a spy working for Francis Walsingham, is sent to Italy to find out as much as he can about a supposed Borgia plot against Elizabeth, and it seems that Oliver is having problems with the research into the Italian part of the book. He was saying only the other day that he can't spare the time to go to Italy himself and that he may well have to employ a research assistant. I thought...'

She broke off as the doorbell rang.

'Oh, heavens, they're arriving already.'

There were no nuances of the fine art of entertaining that were not known to Francesca. She mingled with Beatrice's guests with the quiet grace she had inherited from her mother, adding to it the sophisticated polish she had learned from her aunts, keeping the conversational ball rolling, parrying questions that threatened to become too curious and deftly making each person she spoke to feel that she was genuinely interested in what they had to say.

'Who is she?' Oliver Newton asked Elliott, as they stood together by the fire. He had been watching her for the last five minutes, studying the elegant grace of her body, acknowledging that she was an extremely beautiful and skilled woman.

'The god-daughter of some friends of ours. Let me introduce you.'

Oliver had arrived while Francesca was talking to Helen and John Carter, the doctor and university lecturer, and although she had seen him arrive, good manners had dictated that she did no more than give him a brief glance.

Now he was coming towards her with Elliott, and the tiny shock she had experienced on seeing him redoubled. He was not a handsome man, his features were too hard for that, but no woman could ever overlook him. His eyes were the colour of the sea-spray on the wildest parts of the Italian coast, his hair dark enough to belong to one of her cousins.

The thought sprang into her mind that here was a man who would defy God himself to achieve what he wanted; a man who owned no master... no higher authority... no barriers.

'Francesca, allow me to introduce you to a friend of ours, Oliver Newton.'

'Oliver, meet Francesca, C . . .'

'Valera,' Francesca supplied quickly for him, deliberately omitting her title, and introducing herself as she had done to the other guests by extending her hand and saying firmly, 'Please call me Chessie.'

His flesh felt hard and dry, its contact with her own sending a shocking pulse of sensation through her skin that made her pull away from the handshake.

The silver-ice eyes registered her reaction and mocked her for it.

'Chessie?' he questioned, smiling cruelly at her. 'I think not. Francesca suits you much more. Besides, I abhor nicknames.'

His arrogance took her breath away; that and his blatantly obvious desire to hurt her, and, thus challenged, she reacted in a way she herself would never have expected, looking him full in the eyes and saying coolly, 'Since we are hardly likely to meet frequently, I don't think it can really matter how you choose to address me, Mr Newton.' And then she turned her back on him and walked calmly over to the Carters, neither of whom had seen the small by-play, and both of whom welcomed her back enthusiastically.

'Who did you say she was?' Oliver questioned Elliott again, apparently unaffected by her rebuke.

'The god-daughter of some Italian friends of ours.'

'Mm . . . with no husband or lover in tow, and some very expensive tastes, to judge from her clothes. What's she doing here, Elliott?'

'If you really want to know, why don't you ask her?'

Oliver's eyebrows rose, but Elliott wasn't a man to be challenged or disconcerted by the cool stare of those hypnotic eyes.

'Dinner, everyone,' Beatrice announced, opening the drawing-room door.

She had deliberately not placed Francesca next to Oliver, thus making her his partner, but opposite him, and next to John Carter, knowing that the dinner-table conversation which she fully intended to monitor would include the revelation that Francesca was an expert on her country's history, thus giving her a chance to shine as Beatrice fully believed she deserved to do. It would also give Oliver an opportunity to see that she was not only beautiful but intelligent as well.

Oliver had a theory about women, as unfounded as it was unfair, but Beatrice made allowances for him, understanding that much of his bitter cynicism must spring from the cruelty inflicted on him by his ex-wife.

She had learned from friends in the area that Oliver had adored the little girl he had thought was his child, and local opinion was that he could probably have fought a custody case for her and won, but he had refused to adopt such a course of action because, as he had once harshly told Beatrice, not long after her own daughter was born, he had judged it preferable for the child to be with her mother and the man who was truly her natural father than to be with him, no matter how much he might love her.

This was the first time Francesca had attended such an informal dinner party, where the conversation didn't so much flow politely as eddy and swirl in fascinating and challenging torrents that refused to allow her to remain aloof.

In a very short space of time she was explaining to John Carter her intention of embarking on a new career, and at first she was so carried away by her own enthusiasm that she didn't hear the brief sound of derision Oliver Newton made.

He interrupted her enthusiastic flow of plans to challenge directly, 'Forgive me if I seem cynical, Francesca, but surely if your enthusiasm for a career were as great as you are giving us to understand, you would already have forged the beginnings of this career. You are, after all, no newly qualified graduate, on your own admission.'

Francesca sensed the waiting tension of the other dinner guests. The men looked slightly uncomfortable, with the exception of Elliott, whose expression it was difficult to read, but Francesca had the oddest belief that he was silently encouraging her to go on and not give in to what amounted to little more than bad-mannered bullying.

The women on the other hand looked expectant, as though long used to Oliver Newton's challenging statements and looking to her to defend their sex.

It was a challenge she dared not resist...the kind of challenge she would doubtless often have to face in her new life.

'You are quite right,' she agreed in the cool, beautifully modulated voice she had inherited from her father, her English accentless and perfect. 'Unfortunately, until recently, my life was planned to take a different direction.'

'Really? You intrigue me. What kind of direction?'

The rudeness of the man was intolerable. Francesca looked at him coldly, the haughty, dismissing look of her grandfather, but on this man it had no effect. The silver-ice eyes defied the dismissal of hers, demanding that she answer his question.

'I was to have been married,' she told him briefly, 'and, to save you the inconvenience of questioning me further, yes, it was my fiancé who drew back from the marriage.'

Francesca could sense the sympathetic interest of everyone apart from Oliver himself.

'Unfortunate...but hardly grand tragedy,' he told her harshly. 'And so, now, instead of embracing a husband, you have decided to embrace a career. Hardly the action one would have expected from the newly broken-hearted.'

How would she have felt had she actually loved Paolo, on receiving such an insult? As it was she had the greatest difficulty in remaining in her seat, and not reacting to that hard-edged stare by getting up and fleeing the room.

Forcing back every instinctive feminine reaction she possessed, she calmly finished another forkful of food and then said quietly 'It wasn't a love match, but a marriage arranged between our families. It had been agreed when we were quite small that Paolo and I should marry. I see my decision not as that of a broken-hearted victim, but simply that of a person to whom one career avenue is now closed, and who therefore seeks another.'

Beatrice who had been listening to this exchange with growing tension, was thankful to see Henrietta walk into the room ready to clear away the dinner-plates and serve the pudding.

Someone asked Francesca when she had first become interested in Italian history, and Beatrice, not aware of how she had introduced herself to Oliver, interrupted quickly, 'Oh, I expect it was the first time you realised the significance of your family's place in Italy's history, wasn't it, Chessie? The first Duca was a captain in the army of Lorenzo the Magnificent, wasn't he?'

Try as she might, Francesca couldn't stop herself from looking at Oliver Newton. He was sitting there regarding her with a narrow, derisive smile, as though he knew quite well what had led her into concealing her family title.

'Now I begin to understand the arranged marriage,' he told her contemptuously in a low voice that reached only her ears. 'And the beautiful, if artificial manners . . .'

Francesca bit back a sharp retort. She was suddenly weary of sparring with him. He exhausted her, draining her mental energy and challenging her so much at every turn that he seemed to suck her very life-force from her.

The guests didn't linger long after dinner. Francesca excused herself as they were leaving, feeling that Beatrice and Elliott would appreciate some time to themselves. No one could have made her more warmly welcome, but she was conscious at times that she was an intruder in their home, and that Elliott in particular must resent not having his wife completely to himself.

The only person who had not yet left was Oliver Newton, and she gave him a cool nod, refusing to allow herself to be drawn into any further challenging exchanges with him.

From the hallway Oliver watched her climb the stairs.

'Oliver, have you found a researcher yet?' Beatrice asked him, once she was sure Francesca was in her room.

'No, it's proving far harder than you would believe. No one I've interviewed so far has much more knowledge of the period than I have myself. I wish to God I'd not accepted this American deadline, then I'd have time to do the research myself.'

He was frowning heavily, the austere planes of his face thrown into relief by the hall lights.

'Francesca is an expert on Italian history,' Beatrice told him quietly, and then darted a quick look at Elliott, asking for his support.

He gave it to her, albeit a trifle drily. 'Beatrice is right, Oliver. Francesca certainly has the historical expertise you need, but whether or not it would be wise to induce her to give you the benefit of it, I shouldn't like to say.'

'You won't be called on to do so,' Oliver returned hardily. 'You know what I think of women in the workplace, especially career women: they're motivated by two things. Either they're playing at being men, all aggression and ambition, or they're using their supposed careers as a means of finding themselves a meal ticket for life.'

Upstairs, Francesca, who had realised that she had left her handbag in the drawing-room, gave a smothered gasp of outrage, but it was left to Beatrice to say quietly, 'Oliver, you're letting your prejudices show. I'm sure Francesca doesn't fall into either of those categories. Elliott's quite right,' she added lightly. 'Even if you were to offer Francesca the job, I don't think I could advise her to accept it. You were very hard on her this evening. It isn't her fault she was born into a wealthy aristocratic family... nor that her fiancé jilted her practically at the altar. I admire her for what she's trying to do. It can't be easy for her.'

'Why should it be?' Francesca heard Oliver Newton reply savagely. 'Why *should* life mete out to *her* advantages it doesn't mete out to anyone else? So she's been jilted. So what? Her family will find her another husband and she'll go home and marry him as readily as she was prepared to marry the other one, and you won't hear another word about this supposed career. Will they?' he challenged, stepping back slightly so that he could look up the stairs.

He knew she was there. He had known it all the time... Francesca went rigid with mortification, refusing to move from where she stood in the shadow of the landing. *How* had he known she was there?

She heard him laugh sourly and then walk towards the front door.

By the time Beatrice and Elliott had returned from seeing him to his car, she was safely inside her bedroom with the door closed.

Never before in all her life had she come up against such a man. He was more powerful, more challenging even than her grandfather, albeit in a very different way. Her grandfather's autocracy came from generations of ancestors who had believed in their absolute right to do as they wished because of their birth, and to ensure that the family name was upheld as a name to be revered, while Oliver Newton's arrogance came simply from his own belief in himself. She had never come across anyone like him before, and she shivered as she undressed, remembering the dry heat of his palm against her own; the hardness of the bones beneath the flesh . . . the lightning sensation of power that his touch had conveyed.

As she showered she had a momentary and vivid mental image of his hands on her body, and she stood tensely where she was, riveted to the spot, snapping her eyes open to dispel the unwanted vision, ignoring the fierce spray of the shower.

How on earth had it happened, that fierce surge of awareness so completely unfamiliar to her and yet so shockingly explicit? And she didn't even like the man.

Hurriedly she stepped out of the shower and grabbed a towel, rubbing herself dry.

Forget him, she told herself, After all, it was hardly likely that she would see him again. Not if he had anything to do with it, she reflected wryly.

CHAPTER THREE

'I'M SO sorry, Chessie. I feel terrible letting you down like this, but with Dom not feeling well... Do you mind awfully if we postpone our shopping trip for a few days?'

Beatrice's obvious tension lessened a little as Francesca shook her head and reassured her firmly, 'Of course you must stay with Dom. Actually, it's such a lovely day, I wondered if you'd mind if I went for a walk?'

It had occurred to her after Elliott had finished his breakfast and departed for his meeting in London that it might be easier for Beatrice to cope with her fretful and obviously not very well little boy if she didn't have a guest to entertain at the same time.

The approving glance Henrietta cast her as she cleared away the breakfast things confirmed that her judgement was well founded. Dom, who had woken his parents during the night complaining that he had a sore tummy, was now asleep in his mother's arms, but Beatrice herself looked rather pale and tired, as well she might do, Francesca thought sympathetically.

Even with the loving support of a husband like Elliott and the caring assistance of Henrietta, it still could not be easy taking care of two children under school age, one of whom was still a baby and the other, as Francesca had discovered, a very lively three-year-old with a penchant for mischief and a huge watermelon grin.

'A walk ... Oh, yes. There are lovely footpaths round here. If you can hang on for a second, I think we've got a little booklet showing some of them. You'll need to wrap up well, though. There's a very chilly breeze. Oh, and wear some waterproof shoes or boots if you've got a pair.'

Waterproof shoes. Francesca mentally reviewed the clothes she had brought with her: apart from one pair of plain black satin evening shoes, the others were all high-heeled leather pumps by Charles Jourdan; elegant and indeed very comfortable shoes, but most definitely not waterproof.

'I don't think I have anything suitable with me,' she said carefully to Beatrice, not wanting to add to her conscientious and very caring hostess's burden of worry. 'Is there a shop in the village where I might buy a pair?'

'Yes,' Beatrice told her. 'You'll find it next to the Post Office. Tell them you want a pair of waterproof walking boots. Get a pair with a fleecy warm lining. I find they're the best. Would you hold Dom for me, while I go and find that brochure?'

The sleeping child was a heavy weight in her arms. Francesca considered herself reasonably *au fait* with children and their care—living at the heart of an Italian family, it was hard not to be—but it had struck her, as she watched Beatrice with her son, as she saw Elliott's quick frown of concern before he left the house, that the children she was used to seeing were always presented antiseptically clean and beautifully dressed by their nannies; immaculate accessories to their pretty mamas; always well-mannered and schooled.

She had seen other children, of course, running about the streets, playing games, street-wise children with dark, knowing eyes.

Holding Dom, it came to her that, if the wedding had not been called off, she would very probably by now have been carrying her first child. She would have had to have had a son, of course... Her grandfather would have permitted nothing else.

She was not sorry she had not married Paolo, she decided, relinquishing Dom to his mother's arms as Beatrice returned triumphantly handing her a small leaflet entitled 'Village Walks'. As she was only just beginning to realise, there were other ways to live than that stipulated by her grandfather.

She was beginning to wonder if there wasn't more of her mother in her than she had always supposed. She was finding that she rather approved of the British family life, where husband and wife and later on their children had their own home separate from parents, aunts, uncles and grandparents. And she was beginning to appreciate how difficult it must have been for her mother adapting to life at the *palazzo*.

Francesca was just setting out from the village when the doctor's car arrived. Recognising her from the dinner party, she stopped to exchange a few moments of conversation with her and then set off down the drive.

Drifts of leaves whispered drily round her feet, warmed by the sun, and still crisped with a hint of the frost they had had overnight. The hills in the distance were purple-blue and hazily indistinct, the trees that seemed to stretch right across the countryside to their feet, in irregular masses of gold and bronzes, warm patches of colour against the softer backdrop, their foliage a brilliant contrast to the pale blue of the sky.

It was colder than she had anticipated; her pleated, kilt-like skirt and its complementary soft wool sweater was moulded to her body by the force of the wind.

She had brought with her a bright yellow jacket, which picked out the thin yellow stripe on the tartan skirt, fully believing that she would not need it, but now, as she shrugged elegantly into it, she was glad of its protective warmth.

By the time she reached the village, having stopped once or twice to look curiously inside the shuttered gates of the two large houses she passed, wondering to whom they belonged and admiring the avenues of trees that bordered their drives, her face was glowing pink with the cold, her bare hands tingling.

She found the shop immediately. The village was only small, little more than a straggle of pretty Cotswold houses, either side of the main road. There were no other customers in the shop; the woman who came forward to serve her was small and plump with greying hair and a warm smile.

Explaining what she wanted, Francesca sat down and tried on the selection of footwear she was given. In the end she decided on a pair of sheepskin boots dyed dark blue, which toned in with her skirt. They had warm linings and thick, waterproof soles. The woman serving her showed no surprise when Francesca said that she wanted to keep them on, and parcelled up her court shoes, having first admired the quality of the leather.

Outside again, Francesca realised that she needed gloves. The village had only one dress shop, next to an antique dealer's, and Francesca hovered outside the window for a few minutes, her eye caught by a pretty Dresden piece. She had noticed that Beatrice had several similar pieces on display in her own small sitting-room, and it occurred to her that this shepherdess might make the right gift for her hostess when she came to leave.

Having bought her gloves, and studied the shepherdess again, she looked for somewhere to sit while she studied the pamphlet Beatrice had given her.

Beatrice had mentioned the previous day that the village boasted a very popular tea shop, and Francesca soon found it tucked down a narrow ginnel, which opened out into a courtyard, overlooking the river and surrounded by well-kept green lawns.

The tea shop was open and quite busy. In addition to serving tea and coffee, it also sold a wide variety of specialist teas and coffee beans and, as a waitress led her to a table, Francesca sat back and amused herself watching the shop's customers come and go.

She wasn't in any hurry to rush back. If she did, Beatrice would worry because she wasn't able to entertain her, and besides, it was fascinating watching people come and go.

Beatrice had already mentioned to her that the Cotswolds were a very popular tourist area, and now she was seeing the truth of this statement, recognising one or two American accents among the softer local ones.

She drank her coffee piping hot and ate the scone she had ordered. It was fresh and light and the jam was obviously home-made. Francesca enjoyed her food. She had never needed to worry about her weight, but she never ate more than enough to make her feel just pleasantly full.

The pamphlet described several local walks, most of which she rejected as being too long, but there was one which seemed to circle the village and which she judged would take her back to Beatrice's in good time for lunch. After lunch she intended to suggest that Beatrice should have a rest while she looked after the children, but she sensed that it wouldn't be easy to convince her hostess that she would be quite happy spending her afternoon taking care of her children.

She paid her bill and left. The waitress who had served her was delighted by the tip she had left, and commented in the kitchen that she had been really nice as well as beautiful-looking.

Francesca found the path quite easily. It was well signposted, and led down to the river.

She was glad she had taken Beatrice's advice and bought some boots, because in places the path was muddy underfoot. But, well wrapped up against the cold, she was free to enjoy the brilliance of the autumn sunshine and the peace of the countryside. She paused to watch some ducks paddling contentedly in a large pool. Willow trees overhung it on the opposite bank, and a solitary fisherman sat on a camp stool casting his line.

When the path eventually turned away from the river to run across a field, Francesca walked a little faster. Water had always fascinated her, and she had lingered rather longer than had been wise in the cold wind.

The path crossed another field, and then skirted a copse of trees. In the distance she could see a farmer ploughing, leaving a rich, dark furrow behind the tractor, the strident cries of the birds following him, clearly audible on the cold air.

A high hedge encircled the field, the ground rising steeply towards it, so that she couldn't see what lay on the other side, but when she climbed the stile she discovered to her astonishment that the path led not into another field, but what looked like a private garden.

A rash of ancient outbuildings lay ahead of her, and then an inner stone wall with a gate in it.

The part of the garden she was in was laid out in what must once have been vegetable beds. She could see an untidy tangle of fruit canes which looked as though they hadn't been touched in years and which were thickly overgrown with brambles.

The path cut straight through this garden, and she could see a stile set in the hedge at the opposite side of it.

She looked around, and then, not being able to see where else the path might lead, she climbed down and started to cross the garden, feeling very much the intruder.

She was half-way across when the gate in the inner wall opened and a man walked out. He couldn't see her, concealed as she was by the mass of brambles and overgrown canes, but she could see him, and her heart almost stopped as she recognised him.

Oliver Newton. What horrible chance had brought her here to his garden, where she must obviously be trespassing, having left the real path somewhere in the field?

She panicked at the thought of being confronted by him, without really knowing why. It was a totally unfamiliar sensation to her, but one she couldn't ignore.

He was wearing a pair of worn and faded jeans and a thick woollen sweater, and he seemed to be heading for the pile of logs stacked up by one of the outhouses.

She could, she realised now, see a thin curl of smoke from one of the chimneys she could only just discern beyond the inner wall.

She waited until he had turned his back to her, and then darted out of her hiding place, intent on escaping from the garden before he discovered her in it, only she was frustrated in her escape by a trailing bramble which caught her unawares, tearing painfully at the soft skin of her face and making her cry out instinctively as she fought free of it.

Her cry alerted him, and he turned round, frowning, while Francesca, in a thorough panic, made a headlong dash for the stile and safety from the humiliation of being discovered.

He caught her within a few feet of it, and she was chagrined to discover that, while she was panting and out of breath, his chest was barely lifting.

Glaring at him in frustrated defiance, Francesca mutely challenged him to make his accusations. Instead he smiled at her, a mockingly amused smile that made her toes curl, and her body go weak.

'What was all that about?' he asked her drily, without releasing her.

Yes, *he* was quite definitely amused, while *she*... She felt both shaken and angry. Angry with herself for being such a fool, and for not simply calmly confronting him and asking him the way, as any sane person would have done, instead of reacting like that; and shaken because of the way he was smiling at her instead of frowning.

There was nothing else for it. She would have to tell him the truth. She did so with her head held proudly, her eyes defying him to laugh at her or believe her.

'I didn't want you to get the wrong impression. I was out for a walk, and I think I must have lost my way... The path...'

'Which wrong impression?' he demanded, breaking through the latter part of her explanation.

'I didn't want you to think I was deliberately seeking you out...'

'I know it's generally considered an asset for a writer to have a good imagination, but I think I'd have to be paranoid to imagine that! After all, had you wanted to extend our acquaintanceship, there are far simpler and—er—more socially acceptable methods of doing so. Where have you walked from?' he asked her.

She was too surprised to ignore the question.

'The village. If I've trespassed...'

'You haven't,' he told her calmly. 'This piece of land does have a right of way running through it, hence the wall to screen it from the house and the rest of the garden. Look, it's starting to rain. Why don't you come in and have a cup of coffee? You must have had enough by now. I could run you back afterwards, if you like.'

Francesca was astounded and showed it.

'I do have my human side, you know,' he told her directly, watching the play of emotions across her face.

'You surprise me,' Francesca told him, and then flushed, because she was not normally so direct, preferring to hide her real feelings behind the calm good manners she had been taught as a child.

'Yes, I was rather savage the other night. I'm sorry.'

Sensing that she was not going to get any further explanation, Francesca hesitated, looking for an acceptable excuse to get away, but as she hesitated, the clouds she had not noticed massing on the horizon grew ominously heavy and the first drops of rain started to fall.

'Come on,' Oliver insisted, grabbing hold of her arm and hurrying her towards the door. 'Otherwise we're going to get soaked.'

'The logs,' Francesca reminded him.

'They're not important. I've got enough up at the house for now. I just wanted to get away from my desk for a few minutes.'

The house was long and low, and built in stone. It looked the kind of house that had already withstood many centuries of wear and tear and would withstand many more. The rain was already darkening the slate roof when Oliver opened a side door, ushering her inside to a small square hallway.

He had to duck his head to follow her inside. The ceiling was low, the beams dark with age and polish, the plastered walls in between them uneven and glowing softly white. A patterned carpet in traditional reds and creams warmed the starkness of the small room. One tiny window let in a minimal amount of daylight, and Francesca was not surprised that the lights were on.

'This way. You don't mind if we have our coffee in my study, do you? Only I haven't lit the sitting-room fire as yet, and it's rather cold in there. The house's central heating system is rather ancient and inefficient. I find I manage quite well without it, but visitors often complain, especially women. They coo over the quaintness of the place and then can't wait to modernise it.'

'Have you lived here long?' Francesca asked him politely, the stock phrases learned as a child flowing easily to her lips.

'About five years. I rented it at first and then when it came up for sale I bought it. I like the privacy.'

'And the inconvenience of the lack of modern amenities,' Francesca guessed aloud, immediately flushing when she realised what she had said.

'Clever, aren't you?' he responded drily. 'Yes, they do have their advantages. It's this way.'

He ushered her through another low doorway. Stairs led off to the right and to the left a door into another low-ceilinged, beamed room.

A cat was sitting curled up on a rug in front of the open fire. It opened its eyes and yawned when it saw them.

'Sit down,' Oliver told her, indicating one of the two wing chairs in front of the fire. 'I'll go and get the coffee. I shan't be long.'

This room had a thick blue carpet underfoot and a huge desk took up almost a quarter of the room space, as well as all the light from the small leaded windows.

The desk was covered in papers. An electric typewriter hummed as though it had been abandoned in a moment of frustration without being switched off.

To one side of the desk, an entire wall was taken up with bookshelves, all of them full.

There were other books stacked up in piles on the floor, and she glanced at the spines, reading the titles. Almost all of them dealt with various aspects of the sixteenth-century Italy, a period Francesca was particularly familiar with. She went to pick one of them up, recognising the author, wondering how well his book had been translated into English, and as she did so her attention was caught by a silver-framed photograph on the desk.

It held a photograph of a little girl, perhaps two or three years old. She was smiling into the camera, with all the innocence and eagerness of youth. Wondering who she was, Francesca continued to study her, unaware that Oliver had returned and that he was in turn studying her.

'Your coffee.'

He sounded harsh again, and she spun round guiltily.

'I'm sorry...I didn't mean to pry. I saw your books...' She indicated the pile in front of her helplessly. 'I wondered how Montardi's work had translated into English. I was just going to look at it and then I saw the photograph.'

'And, like all your sex, you're curious?'

'No.'

Francesca's denial was instant and honest. Oliver shrugged.

'I'm surprised Beatrice hasn't already told you. She's the child I once thought was my daughter... The child I *loved* as my daughter... until my late ex-wife decided to enlighten me and tell me that in fact she was the child of the man she'd been having an affair with even before she and I married... the man she was in fact leaving me for, since he had finally divorced his own wife. As an American millionaire, he was obviously of far more worth as a husband than a mere struggling university lecturer. I already knew she wanted a divorce, our marriage had never been a success, but I wanted her, and in those days I was idealistic enough to convince myself that that wanting was love. I told her she could have her divorce, but that I intended to keep our child.

' "What child?" she asked me. *We* had no child. *She* had a child, a child fathered by her lover. And so I had to let them both go.'

'Are you... are you still in contact with them?' Francesca asked him. Absurdly, there was a painful lump in her throat. It was ridiculous that she should feel compassion for this aggressive and very cynical man, but she did.

He gave her a wintry look.

'Hardly. They're dead. The three of them were killed in a freeway accident eighteen months after she left.'

And he blamed himself for that...for the child's death, if not for the mother's, Francesca recognised.

'You're familiar with Montardi's work, then?' he asked her, abruptly changing the subject.

'Yes. The sixteenth century is one of my favourite fields of study. It threw up so many fascinating and powerful figures...not just in Italy, but all over Europe. It's odd, isn't it, how when we look back we can quite clearly see these particular bands of time which seem to stand out from the others?'

'You're thinking of the Medicis?'

'Among others. They were a very powerful and corrupt family and yet, despite their power, the tide of events turned against them. I often wonder——' she mused, carried away by her own fascination with the period, only to break off and apologise.

'No. I agree with you,' Oliver told her. 'It's one of my favourite periods as well. As an age skilled in double-dealing and treachery, it has no equal, at least not in European history.' He looked at her and Francesca returned his regard steadily, not sure what he was looking for but determined to withstand his scrutiny.

'Look,' he said at last, 'about the other night...'

'Please... There's no need to apologise,' Francesca interrupted him quickly.

His mouth twitched and then curled into a grim smile.

'I wasn't going to,' he told her. 'I was simply going to say that I believe I made an error of judgement. I'm thirty-five years old, reasonably well established in my chosen field, reasonably comfortably financially placed, although of course, my means in no way compare with those of the di Valeria family's,' he added, letting her know that he was now fully aware of who she was. 'It isn't exactly unknown for my well-meaning, but sometimes meddlesome friends to try their hand at supplying me with the main commodity they believe is missing from my life—a wife,' he elucidated wryly, when Francesca looked blankly at him. 'Admittedly Beatrice and Elliott have never previously been guilty of such interference, but last Friday was a particularly bad day and I wasn't feeling in the best of moods to start out with.'

He glanced at the photograph on the desk, and frowned. Francesca's mouth had gone dry, as much with astonishment that he should choose to reveal his private pain so clearly to her as with the other odd emotion that threatened to close her throat and jerk at her heartstrings.

He would choose that moment to look up and see the confusion and compassion darkening her eyes.

'Katie's birthday,' he told her shortly. 'She would have been ten. As I said, I wasn't thinking logically, otherwise I would have known from the start that Beatrice and Elliott weren't trying to match us up together.'

'I'm sure they would be very pleased to hear that,' Francesca told him, suddenly very angry, although she could not really have said why. 'I, on the other hand, am not. You see, I find it rather offensive that, while you acquit your friends of, as you call it, trying to match us up together, at no point in your conversation have you even thought to indicate that you realise that *I* might have strong objections to such a plan. I assure you,' she told him proudly, tilting her head and glaring at him, her amber eyes fiery with emotion, 'that I am not so desperately in need of a husband that I would allow myself to be thrust unceremoniously into a stranger's arms. Indeed, if I wanted marriage so desperately, my family would be more than happy to find me a husband. There are a good many men who would be happy to marry the granddaughter of the Duca di Valeria—even now . . . even despite the fact that she has been rejected by one prospective husband.'

'But you didn't want that, is that what you're saying?' he said softly, and suddenly the whole direction of their argument altered, as suddenly and devastatingly as the lightning storms that struck the towers of the ancient Valeria fortress in the Apennines. 'What *do* you want out of life, Francesca?'

'Respect . . . my own and other people's,' she told him huskily. 'Satisfaction . . . the kind of satisfaction that comes from fulfilling one's own targets. Friendship . . . the freedom to make my own decisions and the wisdom to take into account the feelings of others when I do so . . .'

'And love?'

The word seemed to hang on the air, although he had invested it with no special intensity.

'I already have that. I have the love of my parents ... my family. If you refer to the ... the romantic love of novels, I have not experienced it ... nor do I think I shall. My nature is not that way inclined.'

'All women's natures are that way inclined,' he taunted her.

Francesca shook her head and stood her ground.

'I do not think so. It is true that my sex yearns for fulfilment ... for perfection even, but the majority of us have far more realistic and generous standards than do men.'

'Mm.' He turned away from her slightly and appeared lost in watching the rain which was pattering against the small windows.

'And sex?' he asked her with his back to her. 'What part does that play in your life, Francesca, or has that careful cotton-wool upbringing of yours ensured that physical desire is an appetite you have not yet learned to appreciate?'

He swung round to look at her, and for the first time she couldn't meet his eyes. This talk disturbed her. It was true that she was as inexperienced and unawakened as he seemed to guess, but surely not just because of her upbringing? Natural inclination must have played its own part in her calm acceptance of her grandfather's dictum that she must go to her bridegroom a virgin.

'Your silence speaks for itself,' he warned her softly. 'Be careful, Francesca. Otherwise you might come across a man who does not realise what it means to be a di Valeria, nor what kind of future you have been reared for. He will take one look at that soft mouth of yours, and another into those golden eyes, and he will not rest until he has possessed himself of every secret pleasure they withhold from him.'

His words disturbed her. She couldn't hide it. Her heart started to pound, her body going rigid with an awareness of him as a man she refused to allow herself to acknowledge. The small room seemed unbearably warm, and she could feel her body growing hot. Her pulses raced, her mouth going dry with a tension that seemed to begin somewhere in the pit of her stomach.

'I must go,' she said unsteadily. 'It's getting late—Beatrice will be worried.'

'I'll get the car out.'

'No, please . . . I'd rather walk.'

'In the rain?' he asked her, his eyebrows climbing.

'I like the rain.' She ignored his disbelieving look, half afraid that he wasn't going to let her go. And what, after all, was there to be afraid of? she asked herself ten minutes later when she was back on the footpath, shivering a little in the chilly breeze, and all too conscious of how silly she had been not to accept his offer of a lift.

She arrived back later than she had planned, but Beatrice greeted her with a face wreathed in smiles. Dom, it seemed, was a lot better, and the doctor thought he had been suffering from nothing more than a minor tummy complaint.

She asked Francesca how she had enjoyed her walk, and Francesca told her, feeling slightly awkward as she stumbled over her explanation of how she had found herself in Oliver's garden and how she had tried to escape without him seeing her.

'And he caught you as you were trying tactfully to disappear. Oh, poor you!'

'He invited me in for coffee. We had a chat...' And then, in case her hostess got the wrong idea, Francesca added hastily, 'I think he wanted to make it clear to me that he wasn't in the market for a second wife.' She gave Beatrice a wry smile. 'It seems he rather got the wrong impression the other night, for which he blames the fact that it was or would have been the birthday of the little girl——'

'Oh, of course,' Beatrice interrupted in remorse. 'Oh, no wonder he was in such a savage mood. Oh, poor Oliver. He told you about her, then?'

'Briefly. Her photograph was on his desk.'

'He invited you into the inner sanctum? You *are* honoured... of course, it all took place a long time before we knew him. His wife was an American girl he met while he was lecturing in the States. He used to be a university lecturer, you know, but he gave it up when he started to write. Anyway, he met her in the States and married her within a month of meeting her. It was either that or be parted from her, I understand. He didn't want to live permanently in the States and she couldn't get a work permit to come over here unless they were married. She was a secretary, I believe. Anyway, they got married, and from all accounts both of them regretted it right from the start, only she was pregnant and Oliver refused to countenance a divorce once he knew there was going to be a child.

'What he didn't know was that the child had been fathered by her then lover—her boss, who was already married to someone else, and who had refused to get a divorce. Out of pique, Kristie married Oliver.

'Anyway, it seems that Carl, Kristie's lover, had second thoughts and, two and a half years after Kristie and Oliver got married, he suddenly turned up over here to announce that he was divorced and that he wanted Kristie and their child.

'He was a lot older than Kristie, thirty years at least, and there hadn't been any children from his first marriage. By this stage Oliver was ready to agree to the divorce, but he had no idea that Katie wasn't his child until Kristie dropped her bombshell. It seems that, although he didn't want to lose her, Oliver thought she was too young to be separated from her mother, and once he knew that Carl was her natural father... Well, for her sake, he decided that he would have to let her go.

'The three of them were killed less than eighteen moths later, and it was a few years after that that Oliver moved here. The first few months he lived here he lived like a hermit, I believe. No one ever saw him. He had a regular order of groceries delivered every week, and someone went up from the village to clean for him. He produced three novels in three years and brought himself close to the edge of a nervous breakdown.

'We've only known him since we've lived here, of course, and despite that tough exterior, he can be a very kind and compassionate man. There isn't a village charity he doesn't subscribe to. The vicar's wife says he's the softest touch there is when it comes to giving to a worthy cause, but he does have his blind spots, and marriage is one of them.

'I believe there was a concerted attempt among his friends to try and matchmake for him in the earlier years after his divorce, but I think everyone's come to accept now that he doesn't want to marry. I'm sorry if you were embarrassed, Francesca. That was certainly not my intention.'

'Although you did think it would be a good idea if he would give me a job?'

'Yes,' Beatrice agreed flushing a little. 'I'm sorry about that.'

'There's no need... I know you meant well.'

A wail from upstairs caught their attention.

'Ah, I believe my son is awake and hungry,' Beatrice said in some relief.

CHAPTER FOUR

THE telephone shrilled, interrupting Oliver as he worked. He frowned as he put down the dictaphone that he was using and reached the receiver. He wasn't entirely pleased to hear his agent's voice on the other end of the line.

'Yes, Charles, what is it?' he demanded tersely.

'Your American publishers have been on the phone. They want to bring the publication date for your new book forward so that it can be timed to coincide with a very big festival they're holding in New York to celebrate the Italian influence on present-day American culture. Their feeling is that if your book is published during this event, sales will almost certainly at least double.'

Oliver sighed and bit back the curse springing to his lips.

'Charles, you know it's already going to be damn near impossible for me to meet the original deadline, never mind producing the book in even less time.'

'So you still haven't found anyone to help you with the research?' Charles interrupted him. 'Look, why don't you let me got hold of someone for you?'

He could almost feel Oliver's resistance to his suggestion, even down the telephone wire, and wondered despairingly if his most prestigious author was about to display his notorious stubbornness and threaten to stop writing the book altogether, but to his relief Oliver merely said irately, 'No, no, don't do that. I think I can sort something out myself.'

'It looks as if you've got a visitor,' said Francesca to Beatrice as they stood in the garden watching the sleek Daimler turn down the drive towards them.

'That's Oliver's car,' Beatrice replied to her in some surprise. 'That's odd. He doesn't normally make unheralded visits, especially when he knows Elliott isn't here.' She pulled a wry face. 'He's very much a man's man, and really more Elliott's friend than mine. I wonder what he wants.'

If she was aware of the way in which Francesca hung back a little, she didn't betray it, and so Francesca was forced to increase her reluctant speed in order to catch up with her as Beatrice hurried towards the now stationary car. Francesca was disturbed by the way her heartbeat seemed to treble as she watched Oliver extricate his lean length from inside the vehicle. She felt ridiculously short of breath in a way which was not warranted by her brief walk.

'Oliver, what a lovely surprise,' Beatrice commented, greeting him warmly, 'but I'm afraid if it's Elliott you've come to see, he isn't here. He had a business meeting in London this morning and he won't be back until much later.'

'As a matter of fact, it wasn't. It was Francesca.' He looked past Beatrice and directly at her, and her muscles quivered from the strain of holding her body immobile beneath the searchingly intimate look he gave her. A look which was surely not merited by the brevity of their acquaintanceship, and a look which Beatrice had not missed nor failed to interpret, to judge from the rather surprised and speculative way in which she was now looking at her.

'I should have called before now,' Oliver commented, still looking at Francesca, 'to apologise for not driving you home the other day, but as you know, my work has been causing me one or two problems recently.'

'There was no nccd,' Francesca assured him, astonished to discover that she felt almost flustered and that she was reacting as naïvely as a very young girl. It seemed ridiculous when she thought of the sophistication of the life she had lived at home, but there was something about this man that disturbed her—more than disturbed her, she recognised.

'I haven't merely come to apologise for my churlishness,' Oliver continued, giving her a smile which Beatrice later described to Elliott as one which would have cracked icebergs at fifty feet. Francesca steeled herself against the slow, curling heat of it, refusing to acknowledge both to him and to herself the effect that he was having on her senses. It made her angry that he should deliberately employ such a weapon against her. He was no inexperienced youth, and he must be perfectly well aware of the effect of that smile.

'I have a favour to ask you,' he continued, as though unaware of her rigid resistance to him.

'Look, why don't I go inside and make us all a cup of coffee?' Beatrice interrupted hastily. 'You two obviously have private matters to discuss.'

'No,' Francesca interjected harshly, causing Beatrice to give her a worried look. 'I'm sure Oliver has nothing private he wishes to discuss with me.'

'Not private, exactly,' Oliver agreed calmly, 'but I must admit that a cup of coffee would be welcome, Beatrice, if it isn't too much trouble.'

'Not at all,' she assured him. 'Why don't you and Francesca go into Elliott's study, and I'll come and join you when I've made us a drink? I've got to get the children inside anyway,' she continued smoothly when Francesca started to protest.

Francesca watched her walk away, taking the two children with her, and felt as though her last ally was deserting her. She had no idea what it was about Oliver that made her feel like this. He was, after all, no more arrogant and sure of himself than her grandfather, no more sexually aware than many of the men she numbered among her acquaintances.

She moved restlessly from one foot to the other, ill at ease with her own thoughts. A sudden cool breeze caused her to shiver, and gave Oliver the opportunity to walk over to her, removing his jacket as he did so.

'If you prefer to do so, there's no reason why we shouldn't discuss our business out here,' he told her calmly, 'but you'd better borrow this, otherwise you're going to be frozen.'

The soft tweed of the jacket carried his scent and she was preternaturally aware of it, every sense heightened by his proximity, in a way that made her tremble inwardly, like the dove sensing the presence of the hawk. She almost thrust the jacket back at him, in a rare, clumsy gesture that was very untypical of her, and Beatrice, who was watching them from the sitting-room window, frowned and gnawed at her bottom lip worriedly, guiltily conscious of Elliott's warning to her that she wouldn't be doing Francesca any favours in bringing her to Oliver's attention.

'I think we'd better go inside,' Francesca told him stiltedly. 'Beatrice will be wondering where we are.'

The look he gave her showed her that he was aware of her fear and of the reason for it. It rubbed against already raw nerves. The awareness of him, coming as it had done almost out of the blue, was still something she hadn't come to terms with. At first it had surprised and almost amused her, her view of it both slightly detached and disbelieving. As time had passed, and her body had refused to stop its impulsive leaping every time the thought of him touched her mind, she had become less detached and more concerned.

Why, of all times, should her body choose now to remind her of its femininity? Why should desire touch her now when it had never touched her before? Why should this man have the power to unleash such turbulent feelings and emotions within her when no other had?

Francesca did not yet know the answer to these questions, but what she did know was that to allow such feelings to become any stronger would be very, very dangerous indeed. Even so, her upbringing was such that she couldn't refuse to allow Oliver to usher her inside and into the study that was Elliott's private preserve.

It was a very masculine room, with pine-panelled walls and a dark green carpet. It suited Oliver, but it made her feel very vulnerable and weak.

'What is it you want to discuss with me?' she asked him nervously, refusing to look at him.

'I had my agent on the telephone this morning. My American publishers want to bring forward the publication date of my new book. That will be impossible unless I can find someone to help me with the research on it.'

'I thought you always did your own research,' Francesca commented without looking at him.

'I prefer to, yes, but in this instance... In this instance, I was hoping that you would agree to help me.'

That made her turn round and look at him, her golden eyes scornful and just a little afraid.

'After what I heard you saying about my sex—about me to Beatrice and Elliott——'

'I've already apologised for that,' Oliver told her evenly, 'and tried to explain why I reacted as I did. You know,' he commented, idly giving her a mocking smile, 'you are very much the granddaughter of the Duca di Valeria when you stand there looking at me like that, and yet I thought you'd come here to England in an attempt to break away from your background, to find yourself, as it were, and develop your own life. I am offering you an opportunity to do that, Francesca, an opportunity to find out if a life as a researcher is what you want. Or are you afraid?' he suggested softly.

'Of you? Never,' Francesca spat at him, watching his eyes change colour and his body tense like an animal about to spring on its prey.

For a moment she was almost physically afraid of his maleness, and then suddenly the threatening anger left him and he smiled again.

'Of me? Good heavens, no, why on earth should you be? What I meant was, were you afraid that you may not be able to meet the challenge that I am offering you? That you might, after all, be nothing more than another beautiful socialite pretending that she wants a career.'

Francesca felt her skin tingle with embarrassed heat. How neatly he had trapped her, and how very aware he was of that fact. She hated him then, in that moment, and was torn between her natural caution which urged her to refuse to accept his challenge, and the stronger and extremely disruptive emotion which demanded equally strongly that she flung caution to the winds, accepted his job and made him eat those words of mocking contempt he had just uttered.

'Well?' Oliver prompted softly, his smile changing to a frown as they both heard Beatrice outside the door. She came in with Henrietta who was carrying a tray of coffee.

'Oh, dear, have we interrupted at a bad moment?' she apologised, looking from Oliver's set face to Francesca's defiant one.

'Not really,' Oliver told her, stepping forward to take the tray from Henrietta and put it down on the coffee-table. 'I've just been trying to persuade Francesca to come and work for me. My American publishers want to bring forward the publication date of the new book, which means that I have to have help with the research. From our conversation the other day, I gained the impression that Francesca has exactly the kind of knowledge about the period that I most need.'

'Oh, but Oliver, Francesca's come here for a rest, not to work,' Beatrice protested, quickly sensing Francesca's distress and wanting to protect her instinctively.

'I'm not about to kidnap her and force her to work for me,' Oliver told her drily. 'The decision can only be hers. I'll give you the rest of the day to think it over,' he told Francesca, turning to look at her. 'You'll appreciate that because of the timescale involved I can't afford to allow you any longer.'

He reached into his jacket and produced a card on which he scribbled down a telephone number.

'This is the number of my private line,' he told her, handing her the card. 'Perhaps when you've had an opportunity to think things over you'll give me a ring and give me your decision.'

She ought to tell him that she had already made her decision, Francesca acknowledged, as her fingers took the small piece of card. So why was she not doing so? Why was she allowing herself to hesitate and, moreover and more importantly, why was she allowing him to see the hesitation? She was like a child, fascinated by something she sensed was dangerous; without the wit or the common sense to remove herself from that danger.

Oliver drank his coffee quickly and then took his leave of them.

'What will you do?' Beatrice asked Francesca after they had both watched him drive away.

'I don't know. It would be a marvellous opportunity to extend my previous experience—professionally, I mean,' she added, catching the look in Beatrice's eyes.

'I wonder if a professional relationship is all he has in mind,' Beatrice mused in a troubled voice. She looked directly at Francesca and said quietly, 'I feel that I'm to blame for all this. It did occur to me before you arrived that working for Oliver would be an ideal opportunity for you. But that was before . . .' She checked and broke off, looking uncomfortable.

'Before you realised that, for a woman of my age, emotionally I'm very inexperienced,' Francesca supplied for her.

'Oliver has a certain reputation,' Beatrice said hurriedly. 'Not of having a long string of affairs with women, don't misunderstand me. In fact, according to local gossip, his affairs are relatively few and far between, but affairs is exactly what they are, Francesca. He's a very physically sensual man. No woman could be unaware of that, but he's also a man who appears to have decided to live his life without any kind of emotional commitment in it whatsoever. You are a very beautiful and vulnerable woman.'

She gave her guest a very compassionate look. 'Please don't think I'm trying to tell you how to live your life, or that I'm trying to say that if you do decide to work for Oliver, an affair will automatically develop. He certainly isn't the kind of man who would ever use force to constrain a woman into a sexual relationship with him that she didn't want.'

'But you're afraid that I might want that kind of relationship with him,' Francesca submitted, 'and that I might be stupid enough to believe that because he could enjoy making love with me, he might want to make an emotional commitment to me.' She shook her head. 'I'm not that naïve, Beatrice.'

'But you are afraid of agreeing to work for him,' Beatrice insisted.

'Yes, but I still intend to do so.' Until that moment she hadn't even realised herself that she was going to accept Oliver's challenge. 'I have to do it,' she added. 'If I don't, I'll never know whether Oliver is right or not.'

'About what?' Beatrice asked her curiously.

'About whether I have what it takes to make a place for myself in the world, or whether, as he suggests, I'm simply playing at being independent. As for the rest,' she gave Beatrice a direct look, 'I'm not under any illusions, and I have no intentions of complicating my life even further by getting involved with a man like Oliver.'

'Well, if you're sure,' Beatrice said doubtfully, and then added, 'Look, why don't you leave making your final decision until Elliott comes home?'

Francesca gave her a fond look, but said firmly, 'That was a kind thought, Beatrice, but no. I can't spend the rest of my life relying on others to advise me how to live it. I have to make my own decisions and I have to stand by them, right or wrong.'

Beatrice gave a faint sigh, but she didn't make any further protest. Francesca waited until mid-afternoon before making her telephone call to Oliver. He answered on the fourth ring, saying his name with an abruptness that for a moment almost robbed her of the courage to speak. However, she managed to conceal her nervousness with the cool tone of her voice.

She would work for him as his researcher, she
told him, but she felt that a trial period of one week
on both sides would be a safeguard to ensure that
neither of them became trapped in a situation which
was mutually disadvantageous.

'I agree,' Oliver told her, and then added, 'Look,
if you're not doing anything this evening, why don't
we have dinner together and we can discuss the way
I work, the sort of information I'm going to need,
salary and all that kind of thing?'

'I'll have to check with Beatrice,' Francesca told
him, 'but if she has nothing planned, then yes, I
think that would be a good idea.'

She already knew that Beatrice did not have anything planned for the evening, but she wanted to
keep her relationship with Oliver on a firmly
business footing, and therefore she made this show
of going to check with Beatrice before going back
to the telephone and informing Oliver that she
would be able to see him.

'Excellent. I'll pick you up at about eight o'clock.
Mrs Lyons who comes in from the village to clean
for me, will probably organise a meal for us, and
then we can spend the rest of the evening discussing
how we're going to work together.'

It was too late for Francesca to protest that she
hadn't realised when he invited her out for dinner
that he intended them to dine in his own home. She
felt as though she had been deliberately led into a
trap, although she wasn't able to explain to herself
why. After all, what did it matter where they discussed the terms of her employment with him?

It didn't, and yet, as she replaced the receiver, she had the feeling that he was very well aware of her unease and of the reason for it.

Realising that Francesca was not going to change her mind, Beatrice forbore suggesting to her again that she wait to make her final decision until after she had discussed the whole thing with Elliott. However, after Oliver had arrived to collect Francesca, and the pair of them had driven off, she couldn't help confiding to Elliott how concerned she was.

'I thought that was what you wanted,' Elliott commented mildly. 'The whole idea of last week's dinner party was to get the two of them together, wasn't it?'

'Only because I thought they could help one another,' Beatrice assured him. 'Oh, Elliott, you didn't see the way he looked at her this morning.'

'I think I can imagine,' he told her drily. 'Francesca is an extremely beautiful young woman.' He saw her face and hastened to reassure her, 'Ah, no, my love, I speak only in the abstract. She is a beautiful woman, but you must know that in my eyes no one could ever be as beautiful as you.'

'She's no match for him, Elliott,' Beatrice fretted, after she had allowed herself to be placated with this blatant piece of flattery.

'Stop worrying,' Elliott told her. 'She's an adult, Beatrice, and quite capable of telling Oliver that she wants their relationship to be on a purely business footing, always providing that he offers her an alternative and she chooses to reject it.'

'Oh, Elliott,' Beatrice reproached him. 'Life is never as cut and dried as that. You know that. What worries me is that Francèsca might fall in love with Oliver. After all, he's a very attractive man.'

'Oh, he is, is he?' Elliott remarked drily, causing her to laugh and shake her head at him in mock reproof.

Meanwhile the couple under discussion had already reached Oliver's house. He helped Francesca out of his car with a courtesy she had not really anticipated, but the warmth of his palm beneath her elbow possessed a far more raw masculinity than the similar attentions of her countrymen. There was something about this man that was raw and untamed: a dangerous fascination to which she suspected very few members of her sex would be immune.

They had approached the house at a different angle from that which she remembered, and now parked outside the front door. Oliver had to duck beneath the thin tendrils of wistaria as he unlocked it to let them both in.

'Mrs Lyons had left everything ready for us. The dining-room's this way,' he told her, once again sliding his palm under her elbow. She could feel the warmth of it through the thin wool of her dress, and for some quixotic reason that heat made her shiver. Even in the dimness of the hallway she saw his smile, its intense male quality making her tense, every inch of her skin prickling with defensive resentment.

'You know, you've rather surprised me,' he told her as he opened the dining-room door for her. 'I half expected you to refuse to have dinner with me once you realised we would be dining here.'

Once again Francesca tensed, but this time her tension was caused wholly by irritation. She turned to face him, her eyes signalling her feelings.

'I came here tonight to discuss a potential business arrangement,' she told him coolly, and then, holding his glance with her own, she added firmly, 'Forgive me if I've been remiss, but I didn't think it was necessary for me to state that this is the only kind of relationship I want to discuss.'

Was that respect she saw creep into his eyes, edging out the mockery she had seen there earlier?

'Good. I'm glad you're not afraid to speak plainly when you feel you need to,' he told her approvingly, and Francesca had the feeling that she had just passed an unsuspected test. What had he been testing her on? Her vulnerability to him?

He was a very attractive man, she admitted inwardly, and one who had his own reasons for not wanting any emotional involvements. Had he thought, perhaps, that she might have taken the job with him because she was attracted to him? And yet this morning he had given her every encouragement to believe that he found her physically attractive—another trap? She wasn't sure.

'Perhaps we both ought to lay our cards on the table,' she said coolly. 'I am taking this job because I know that it will stretch my abilities and help me to form a much clearer impression of whether or not I can make a career for myself as a researcher. I should have applied the same criteria to whether or not to take the job had you been a member of my own sex.'

It wasn't strictly true. Had the job offer come from another woman, she would have accepted it without the slightest hesitation. She knew that.

He gave her a very shrewd look, but made no comment other than to say, 'I appreciate your honesty. It's a very rare commodity in your sex, or so I've found.'

'Men are just as good at deception as women,' Francesca pointed out to him quickly.

'Shall we call a truce?' he asked her, smiling at her.

A sudden spurt of courage gave her the impetus to say, 'Yes, but only if you tell me first why you worked so assiduously this morning to give me the impression that you found me...'

'Attractive, desirable...' he supplied wryly for her, causing her poise to desert her briefly beneath the look he gave her. 'I didn't have to work at it,' he assured her forthrightly, and then added, 'Very well, perhaps I was guilty of, shall we say, making my awareness of you rather more obvious than was perhaps necessary, but...'

'But you wanted to see how I would react,' Francesca challenged him. 'You wanted to see if I was stupid enough not to see what lay behind your flattery,' she added.

'Maybe,' Oliver agreed non-committally, 'or maybe I wanted to see why such a very beautiful woman should be so very obviously disturbed by a man's interest in her. Please don't tell me, Francesca that you haven't excited male interest almost from the day you entered puberty, because I shan't believe it.'

Her anger manifested itself in the look she gave him.

'I was three years old when my grandfather decided that Paolo and I would marry,' she told him frostily. 'I grew up with that knowledge, and because of that...'

'And because of that you shut yourself off from the rest of the male sex?' he questioned her disbelievingly. 'No wonder you have such a feeling for history, Francesca. You're practically medieval yourself.'

Her eyes flashed their warning again, and he wondered if she had any idea of how stunningly beautiful she was. She was unlike any other women he had ever known. Her upbringing had given her a patina of sophistication and experience that he was only just beginning to realise was nothing more than a patina.

He wondered about her grandfather; about the mind and the heart of a man who could decree that his granddaughter should be used to further his own ambitions. The di Valeria family could trace its roots back to the fourteenth century and beyond, and it seemed that the blood that had run so hotly in those Machiavellian medieval princes still ran strongly in the veins of some of their descendants.

He wondered what her grandfather had planned for Francesca now, how long he would allow her the illusion of imagining that she was free. She looked at him, and her soft, full mouth throbbed with the fierce pride of her eyes. She would be a challenge to any man, and he wondered a little about her fiancé, who had rejected her in favour of somebody else.

None of the thoughts running through his mind were betrayed in the look he gave her as he indicated one of the chairs and invited her to sit down.

'Mrs Lyons has left us a chicken casserole. I'll just go and get it,' he told her.

For all her English blood, Francesca's Italian heritage had a strong hold on her. It was not easy to forget the early training of her many aunts, who had taught her young that it was a woman's duty to see to the comforts of the men of her family above and beyond everything else.

'I'll come with you,' she told him, and was in the kitchen before he could stop her. She had the lid off the casserole and was delicately exploring its flavour. It was pleasant enough, but a little bland for her own personal taste. Had she the contents of the *palazzo* kitchen to hand, she would very soon be able to transform this plain English food into something with far more verve and flair.

Oliver watched her curiously. She was a creature of strange contrasts, odd and totally unexpected quirks. Here in his kitchen, she was so totally at home and at ease that it was hard to remember that she was a woman who was very probably a millionairess in her own right; a woman who most certainly did not need to work for her living, and even more certainly would surely never in her life have been required to taste the contents of the *palazzo* kitchen stockpot.

She looked up and saw him, and as though she had read his mind she told him simply, 'All Italian women are taught from birth that, above and beyond everything else, their home and the people in it must be their first concern. My mother found it very hard when she first married my father. She has told me since that it took her a long time to realise that she had married not just a man, but an entire family.'

'And yet you seem to have adapted to the British way of life quite easily.'

Francesca shrugged her shoulders and sighed, replacing the lid on the casserole, realising that it was pointless yearning for the herbs of the kitchen at home.

'My mother has told me a lot about this country. She and my father have English friends whom we have visited on many occasions.'

She wasn't going to tell him what her mother had confided in her shortly before she left, and that was that, despite all the Duca's plans for his granddaughter, her mother had always hoped that somehow or other the marriage would be prevented and Francesca would be given the opportunity to make her own way in life and to choose for herself the person that would share that life with her. Now it seemed that the first part of her mother's wish at least had come true. As to the second, Francesca was not totally sure that she wanted to share her life with anyone else. She was only just beginning to discover the pleasure of being in full control of it herself, and there *was* a pleasure in that, even though it might be a faintly frightening one.

This afternoon, for instance, when she had made her decision to work for Oliver, she had been very aware of her grandfather's probable reaction to what she was going to do. None of the di Valera women had ever worked other than inside their homes, taking care of their husbands and raising their children. He had been completely against Francesca's receiving the education she had done, and it had only been because Paolo's mother had supported her own parents that he had allowed Francesca to go on to university.

No, her grandfather wouldn't be pleased at all. And another thing that wouldn't please him would be the fact that she was working for a man who was unknown to him. Her grandfather had very strict and old-fashioned views; too strict and old-fashioned, Francesca decided rebelliously.

'What's wrong?' Oliver asked her drily, watching the vivid play of emotions cross her face. 'Isn't the casserole to your liking?'

'It's fine,' she assured him, guiltily aware that her thoughts were showing so plainly on her face.

'Perhaps we'd better go and eat it, then, and while we do we can discuss the most efficient way for us to work together.'

It was agreed that Francesca should arrive at ten o'clock in the morning for the first couple of weeks, and that Oliver would instruct her as to the exact nature of his requirements so that she could spend the afternoons involved in the research he needed while he got on with his actual writing.

'We'll have to share the study, I'm afraid,' he told her. 'All my reference books are there, anyway. I use a dictaphone most of the time, but if that disturbs you, you can always get the books you need and take them through into the sitting-room and extract the data I require in there.'

Before she left, he gave her a copy of the opening chapters of his book and a draft of the outline.

'I already know the basic personalities of the main characters,' he told her briskly, 'but what I need now is the information to flesh them out. What I also need is a good deal of accurate historical background information. Once you've read through the outline, you'll have a clearer idea of what I mean. The main character is an English man, a spy, working for Francis Walsingham. He is sent to Italy to discover what he can about a Medici plot to assassinate Elizabeth. The main female character is a girl who is a ward of the Medicis; a fascinatingly corrupt family, the Medicis,' he remarked.

'Not all of them,' Francesca pointed out.

He looked at her sharply. 'Perhaps not, but for the purposes of my novel, it would be the corrupt members of the aristocracy whom I wish to highlight.'

'Cesare Borgia?' Francesca asked him.

'Yes, and Queen Catherine.'

'I've always felt rather sorry for her,' Francesca remarked. 'It must have been terrible to have loved somebody the way she did, and yet to know that, although she was his wife, her love would never be returned. She must have hated his mistress, Diane de Poitiers.'

They were soon so deep in a historical discussion that Francesca could hardly believe it when Oliver remarked that it was half-past twelve, and if he didn't get her home soon Beatrice would be panicking like a mother hen.

It was gone one o'clock when he drove up to the house. He got out and escorted her to the door, a courtesy that Francesca hadn't expected. His sleeve brushed her arm as he rang the bell, and a tiny shiver of sensation shot through her. This awareness of him was something she was going to have to combat, Francesca warned herself, as Elliott let them both in. It could only complicate their relationship and make her vulnerable.

Having ensured that she was safely inside, Oliver showed no inclination to linger.

'I'll see you in the morning at ten, then,' he told Francesca.

'So it's all settled,' Elliott commented after Oliver had gone.

'Yes, I start work for him tomorrow. Initially just for a week while we see how things work out.'

She had the feeling as she went upstairs that she was taking a momentous step forward; a great leap into the unknown. But whether or not it was a wise step, only time would tell.

CHAPTER FIVE

UNDRESSED and ready for bed, Francesca blessed the thoughtfulness of a hostess considerate enough to provide her house-guests with a comfortably padded upright chair and a solid flat-topped desk to go with it.

Beatrice had explained to her that the desk also served as a breakfast table for those guests who preferred to eat their first meal of the day in the comfort of their own room.

'My godfather, who is in his late sixties now, says he can't face the hurly burly of modern family life until at least eleven o'clock in the morning and after several cups of Henry's coffee,' she had added with a grin.

Francesca had no desire to eat in the solitude of her room. In fact, rather to her surprise, she was enjoying living *en famille* with Beatrice and Elliott in a way she had never experienced during her years at the *palazzo*, which had been overflowing with aunts, uncles, cousins of every degree.

Perhaps that was because by the time her grandfather had finally prevailed upon her father to return to the family home she had already been five years old, and because of her English blood and her upbringing she was already set apart from the other children.

Add to that the fact her brothers were away at school and that none of her cousins had been close

enough to her in age for any close friendship to
form, and it was perhaps easy to understand why
she had always held herself a little remote from
them. She had sensed, even as a child, that the
family did not entirely approve of her mother, the
English girl who had stolen the heart of the Duca's
eldest son and whom he had married despite all his
father's protests.

It was very late when she finally went to bed. She
had read the papers Oliver had given her not once,
but twice. He was a very powerful, magnetic writer,
his dialogue sharp and succinct for all its medieval
flavour, his characters drawn with bold, strong
strokes so that they sprang vividly to life in front
of her.

She wondered how much of Oliver there was in
his main character, the spy, Kit Faversham. She
learned in the early pages of the manuscript that it
was the death of his wife which had led him to
rejoin Francis Walsingham's secret army of spies,
this no doubt being Oliver's method of resusci-
tating his hero. Oliver had already told her that
originally he had not intended to write a second
book featuring Kit, but that the first one had been
so popular that his agent had begged him to try.

She would need reference books, she reflected
drowsily when she eventually went to bed. With
Beatrice's permission, she would telephone her
mother in the morning and ask her to send some
over. She already owned most of the volumes she
would need. Sleepily, she yawned and then closed
her eyes.

* * *

'Ring Italy—yes, of course you may,' Beatrice agreed willingly when Francesca asked her. 'Why don't you use the telephone in my sitting-room? Elliott is working at home today, otherwise you could use his study. You're definitely going to work for Oliver, then?'

'I think so. We've agreed on a trial week on both sides to see how it works out, which reminds me; I'd better hurry, otherwise I'm going to be late.'

Beatrice diplomatically accepted that the subject was closed, and Francesca took her coffee into the small pretty sitting-room which was Beatrice's own private preserve.

A little to Francesca's annoyance, her uncle Marco answered the telephone. Married to her father's eldest sister, he was a small, fussy man, who could never resist interfering in the affairs of others. Only his enormous wealth and the fact that he had five other daughters to find husbands for had persuaded her grandfather to permit the marriage, and Marco was now almost as zealous of the family name and honour as the Duca himself.

It was several minutes before her mother came to the telephone, and Francesca pictured her hurrying down the long, draughty corridors of the *palazzo*, her face flushed, and the soft blonde hair which her father loved so much in disarray.

'Darling, how are you? Is everything all right?'

'Everything's fine,' Francesca assured her. 'I've got a job... working for a writer as a researcher. A friend of Beatrice and Elliott's,' she added reassuringly, anticipating her mother's questions. 'I need some of my books, *mamma*,' she told her. 'If

I give you a list, could you send them to me, please?'

In the end, the telephone call lasted rather longer than she had planned. She must make sure that she found some way to recompense Beatrice for the cost of it, although she doubted that her hostess would allow her to give her the money. Perhaps a gift for the children...Beatrice had remarked only the other day how attractive she found Italian children's clothing.

She dressed warmly for her walk to Oliver's, glad that she had had the forethought to return to the shoe shop and add a pair of smart flat brogues to her original purchase of boots.

Beatrice was concerned to learn that Francesca intended to walk to and from Oliver's every day, and tried to press her own small car on her, but Francesca refused, shaking her head. She knew quite well that Beatrice needed her car for shopping.

'I shall enjoy the walk,' she told Beatrice firmly and truthfully.

'When the weather is fine and dry, yes, but what about when it rains...or snows?' Beatrice protested.

'I shall enjoy those, too,' Francesca assured her.

It was half-past nine, which by her calculations allowed her plenty of time to walk to Oliver's if she took the short cut through the fields and the small copse.

Beatrice watched her go, giving a faint sigh as she admired her calm poise. And it only struck her as she went into the kitchen to make Elliott a cup of coffee that a man like Oliver might get a good deal of satisfaction in breaking through such poise, and she gave a tiny little shiver of apprehension.

Francesca had calculated well. It was just five to ten when she reached the rear gate to Oliver's garden, even though she had lingered on the way to watch some rabbits at play.

There had been a long Indian summer, Beatrice had told her, lasting well into October, and even now the weather was still mild for the time of year, although changes were predicted.

Mrs Lyons, Oliver's cleaner, let her in, her initial suspicion melting away completely when Francesca thanked her for the previous evening's meal.

As Mrs Lyons told her daughter later, 'A real lady she is and no mistake. You can always tell quality, I say.'

Oliver was already working, Mrs Lyons informed Francesca, and she was to go straight through when she was ready.

'The mornings I'm here I always make him a bit of something and take him a cup of coffee at eleven, but I'll do it a bit earlier this morning if you like,' she offered conspiratorially as she watched Francesca remove her jacket and walking shoes, changing the latter for the elegant court shoes she had tucked away in her capacious shoulder-bag.

She had also brought with her a notepad and pen and a small dictaphone which Elliott had offered her, saying that she might find it useful.

'It's amazing the things that occur to one at the most inconvenient times. Keep that with you and use it as an *aide-mémoire*. I think you'll find it very useful.'

Francesca had thanked him, knowing that Elliott's advice, although rarely given, would also be worth taking.

When she walked into the study, she found Oliver deeply engrossed in what he was doing. He was sitting in front of a complicated-looking word processor, typing into it in rapid-fire bursts of impatient words, his forehead creased in a deep frown.

He was so engrossed in what he was doing that he didn't even look up at her, and, sensing that he would not appreciate being distracted, Francesca walked calmly across to the window and, taking care not to obscure all the daylight, sat down behind the table where Oliver had already indicated she was to work, and got out her notebook and the manuscript.

Very quickly she too was totally engrossed in what she was doing, so much so that the entrance of Mrs Lyons with coffee and biscuits startled her almost as much as it did Oliver.

He stopped what he was doing and asked briefly, 'Is it that time already? Hell...'

He pushed his hand into his hair and massaged the back of his scalp as though it ached, his frown deepening.

'I brought the coffee a bit earlier this morning,' Mrs Lyons informed him. 'I thought that Miss Francesca must be cold after that long walk.'

Francesca saw his eyebrows rise at Mrs Lyons formal mode of address.

After she had gone Oliver picked up his coffee and, for a moment, Francesca thought he intended to ignore her altogether, but he got up from behind the word processor and walked over to the window, stretching his spine as he did so, as though his back ached. And if it did, no wonder; there had been tension written into every line of his body when she'd originally walked in, and she suspected that he had been so totally engrossed in his writing that he was almost living through it himself.

'It looks like I've got an embryo witch working for me,' he commented grimly, destroying her comfortable illusion that he was so engrossed in his work that he was barely aware of her. 'You certainly seem to have put Mrs Lyons under some sort of spell... *Miss* Francesca.'

'That was her idea, not mine,' Francesca told him defensively.

'Oh, I don't doubt it.'

The comment was bland enough, but Francesca felt as though the day had started off on the wrong footing. She was sensitively vulnerable both to the mockery in his voice and the suggestion that she was being given preferential treatment.

If she was, it wasn't because she had desired it. Far from it, but how could she explain to him that she had felt obliged to accept it rather than offend Mrs Lyons?

'I've read through the manuscript,' she told him quietly, wanting to change the subject. 'I've also been on the telephone to my mother this morning to ask her to send me the reference books I'm going to need.'

She wanted to tell him how much she had enjoyed what she had read, but she didn't want to be accused of trying to flatter him, or, worse still, told brusquely that since she was not a critic her opinion of his work could scarcely be of any interest to him, and so she kept quiet, sipping her coffee.

'I'm going to give you a list of the main factual Italian characters,' he told her abruptly. 'What I

want from you is as detailed and accurate data as
you can find concerning every single aspect of their
lives, even where it is not relevant to the book, because the more I know about them, the easier it
will be for me to project a believable image of them.
I might not refer in my book, for instance, to the
fact that Cesare Borgia was torturing small animals
when he was a very young child, but it is that kind
of knowledge which will enable me to draw the most
realistic image of the adult man.'

'And if he wasn't... If it turns out that he was
a child much like any other?' Francesca challenged.

'He wasn't,' Oliver assured her tersely.

And there, it seemed, the discussion ended. Fin-
ishing his coffee, he put down the cup and returned
to his own desk.

'Here's a preliminary list,' he told her. 'And in
addition I'm going to need a good deal of factual
background information...the manners and clothes
of the times...the way people lived...the towns
and cities...education...medicine...everything.'

Nodding, Francesca took the list from him. A
good deal of the background information he required was already stored away in her brain, but
she was not going to offer him any facts she had
not checked and rechecked. He had that kind of
effect on her.

It was four o'clock when Oliver spoke to her again.
Lunch had been eaten in silence, as Oliver munched
the sandwiches Mrs Lyons had brought without
lifting his glance from his work.

Francesca had found his total concentration on
what he was doing daunting at first, but then

gradually she had found that she herself was taking inspiration from it, and by mid-afternoon she was as comfortable with his all-absorbing silence as though she had worked with him all her life.

Their arrangement was that for the first week she would work from ten until four, but that her hours would be longer as the work progressed and if they both agreed that the arrangement was to continue.

Not wanting to disturb him, but knowing she had done as much as she could do for one day, she packed away her things quietly and got up.

As she reached the door, he lifted his head and looked at her.

'If you want to hang on for half an hour, I'll run you back.'

Francesca shook her head.

'There's no need. Besides, I'm looking forward to the walk.'

She arrived back just in time to share the children's tea-time with Beatrice, and then over dinner she was able to discuss with both her and Elliott her reactions to her new job.

'It's very challenging,' she told them.

'Because of the work content, or because of Oliver?' Elliott asked her drily.

'Both!' she admitted honestly.

The days flew past. Francesca's books arrived, accompanied by a loving and encouraging letter from her parents. She slept at night dreaming of Oliver's characters. She worked as hard as Oliver did himself, and at the end of the week when he told

her tersely that if she wanted the job it was hers,
she didn't know whether to be pleased or sorry.

He saw the expression on her face and laughed
without humour.

'Yes, I know,' he told her grimly. 'A dilemma,
isn't it? For me as well, Francesca. You are easily
the best researcher it would be possible for me to
find, far outclassing any other potential candidate,
but...'

And that 'but' lingered in her mind long after
she had left him. She had refused to acknowledge
what he was trying to say, and had told him hurriedly that she would take the job.

It wouldn't be for long, after all. A matter of
months, after which she would be fully justified in
calling herself an experienced researcher, and sure
of getting another job...perhaps even under-
taking further study. Only a few short weeks, that
was all... Nowhere near long enough for that sharp
physical awareness of him that refused to go away
to develop into anything that could really threaten
her.

They both knew where they stood. They both
knew the attraction existed, even if only tacitly, and
they were both determined not to allow it to develop, albeit for very different reasons.

No, it was silly to dwell too much on those telling
shivers of sensation that ran through her body like
minor charges of electricity whenever Oliver
chanced to touch her by accident, or those strange
presentiments she would have that he was watching
her, which would cause her to lift her head and find
his gaze concentrated on her with a heart-stopping
mixture of anger and desire.

No. Neither of them was foolish enough to let
that unwanted awareness of the other develop into
something stronger. She, because she did not want
the emotional pain she knew must follow any kind
of physical relationship with Oliver, no matter how
fleeting or intensely satisfying it might be while it
lasted. She was not emotionally built in such a way
as to be able to give herself over into physical satisfaction of the desire she could sense building
between them, without committing herself
emotionally as well, and Oliver, because he was as
aware of that vulnerability within her as she was,
and he had already made it plain to her that he had
nothing to offer her, or any other woman,
emotionally.

Even so, it was disturbing that he should have
been the one to hesitate over continuing their as-
sociation; because surely *she* was the one who had
more to fear from it? And she sensed that the
burden for ensuring that that dangerous attraction
did not burst past the controls they had posted on
it would fall mainly on her shoulders. He was an
experienced, worldly man who would have no hesitation in taking her to his bed should she indicate
to him that she wished him to do so—just so long
as it was on *his* terms. And those terms, as she well
knew, did not include anything other than the mere
physical satisfaction of their mutual desire.

And yet to read his work, to almost feel the
emotional impact of his main characters, was to
feel oneself so in sympathy with their passions that
it left Francesca physically drained.

His hero, made savage and dangerous by the
death of his young wife and child, lured back into

the web of intrigue and danger Francis Walsingham
wove so cleverly, so that as a reader she was still
not sure if it was the plotters against Elizabeth who
had been responsible for their deaths, or
Walsingham himself, in his cold-blooded determination to secure Kit's services.

And then there was Bellengaria, the beautiful
ward of the Medici family, the child who had grown
up surrounded by its vicious and Machiavellian
members. The pawn set by Queen Catherine to trap
Francis Walsingham's spy, she walked an almost
impossible tightrope between pleasing her family in
order to stay alive and remaining true to her own
ideals.

She would fall in love with Kit Faversham, of
course. How could she not do? But he was a man
hardened by the loss of his wife and child, both of
whom he had loved very much, and he had already
told Walsingham that since he had already lost the
only two people who mattered to him, he cared not
whom he might have to sacrifice in order to protect
the Queen. Would he sacrifice Bellengaria if it
became necessary? Catherine had ordered her to
become his mistress. So far she had cleverly re-
sisted her demands by claiming that Kit had rejected her, but time was running out for her.
Already Kit was stalking her through the French
court, determined to discover how many of her
family's secrets she shared. If he had to feed her
false information of his own in order to win them
from her, he cared not; nor what might become of
her when she passed that information on to her
family and was betrayed by it.

Bellengaria, intelligent, sensitive and very much in love, was caught in a dangerous trap, and Francesca was amazed that Oliver should be able to write so tellingly and believably about her emotions.

No... She might not be able to stop those treacherous flutters of sensation weakening her on those rare occasions when he chanced to touch her, nor could she entirely prevent herself from thinking about him when she was on her own, marvelling a little at the depth of emotion he aroused within her—the desire, the compunction to reach out and touch him...to...to know that alien male flesh...to be consumed in the fierce heat that quickened madly inside her and which she fought rigorously to control—but these were weaknesses she managed to ignore during her working hours. It was only at night, when she lay alone in bed, that they tormented her. They were the price she had to pay for working with him, and she paid it gladly, offering up her peace of mind almost as a sacrifice to appease what she knew to be a flagrant flirtation with danger.

And because she thought she *had* appeased it, she told herself that the danger was tamed and controlled and that she was safe.

And then three things happened that showed her how wrong she was.

CHAPTER SIX

THE first came with the abrupt change in the weather. Almost overnight, or so it seemed, the calm, crisp mellowness left the air, and in its place came icy winter winds and heavy squalls of rain that battered at the windows and kept Francesca awake half the night.

In the morning the sky was grey with heavy cloud, the rain had turned the footpath into oozing mud. It clung to her boots and made her legs ache from the effort of walking. For the first time she did not enjoy her walk across the fields to Oliver's house, the harsh wind and beating rain reminding her that she was, after all, a creature of much warmer climes and unused to the raw unkindness of such weather.

She was shivering when she arrived, and as she stripped off her wet coat and muddy boots in the passage alongside the kitchen she was looking forward to a cup of Mrs Lyons' coffee.

Only Mrs Lyons wasn't there!

Her sister was ill, Oliver told her tersely, when she enquired after her whereabouts, and she would be away for several weeks.

Francesca bit her lip, realisingly guiltily that she had interrupted him. He had been tense for the last couple of days, the periods of silence between his fierce clattering of the keyboard gradually growing longer, and more pregnant with tension.

Now the very air in the room seemed to hum with it, and she found herself hardly daring to breathe, in case by doing so she unwittingly sparked off the rage she could sense burning beneath Oliver's surface calm.

At eleven o'clock, she was fighting not to give in to the shivers of cold still convulsing her. The central heating system was fuelled by a boiler which Mrs Lyons normally cleaned out and lit as soon as she arrived in the morning.

Today, of course, this had not been done, and Oliver, it seemed, did not share her awareness of the room's chill. How she longed for a bowl of warming soup, or even a cup of hot coffee—so much so that she knew she was not giving her work the concentration it required, but she dared not move, in case by doing so she exploded the dangerous minefield that was Oliver's fierce concentration.

And then from outside came a loud crash, that splintered the tension and made Francesca almost jump in her seat.

Oliver cursed volubly and pushed the machine back on his desk with such force that Francesca feared it would actually fall on to the floor.

'I'm going out for a walk,' he told her tersely, standing up. 'I need to think.'

She didn't say a word. She had seen the tension mounting for too long. This must be the notorious writers' block she had heard of, and all her innate wisdom warned her to neither do nor say anything that might deflect his concentration.

She watched him leave, studying him covertly. He had gone out in the jeans and shirt he had been working in, only pulling on a thick sweater as added protection and a pair of boots. She saw him disappear in the direction of the vegetable plot and the dilapidated greenhouses, and guessed that the crash must have come from there.

Rather guiltily she waited for him to disappear from sight, and then hurried into the kitchen to find a pair of protective gloves so that she could clean out and reset the fire.

That kept her so occupied that it was some time before she realised how much the force of the wind had increased. It was raining as well, fierce droplets of moisture coming down the chimney and spattering savagely in the flames as the wind gusted smoke into the room.

Once she was sure the fire was going, she put up the fireguard and went into the kitchen. Mrs Lyons was an adequate cook, but nowhere near the same standards as Francesca's mother or aunts. She opened the fridge door and found the carcass of a chicken. It would make a nourishing broth, far more tasty than the canned soup Mrs Lyons insisted on supplying. Beneath the fridge was a small freezer. Francesca opened the door and inspected the contents. When Oliver came back he would probably be hungry, and if he wasn't, then she certainly was.

The freezer was well stocked with a good selection of meat, fish and poultry. Had the cupboards contained the necessary ingredients, she could have made a delicious dish of cannelloni, using her aunt Constantia's favourite pasta recipe, but she doubted that Mrs Lyons had ever eaten pasta in her life, never mind bought the ingredients to make it.

A check of the cupboards proved that she was quite right, and she was amused to discover how much of her aunts' training she had absorbed as she found herself mentally constructing a shopping list and deploring the lack of originality and house-wifely skill exhibited in the cupboard's contents.

In fact, she was so engrossed that it was some time before she realised how long Oliver had been gone, but even then she didn't worry. A walk would no doubt help him to get rid of his tension, and might even ease his mind enough for his thought processes to start working again. She was constantly amazed by the ideas that popped into her own head on her walks to and from her work.

No. It was only when the wet afternoon started to darken towards dusk that fear for him began to edge its way into her mind.

It was gone four o'clock, well past the time when she should leave.

What ought she to do? Wait for Oliver to return? And suppose he didn't want her to? But also suppose something had happened to him while he was out? He could have slipped...hurt himself. This and other equally wild thoughts were racing through her mind when she heard a door bang and realised that he had returned. Not wanting him to think that she had been deliberately awaiting his return, she tidied up her desk and was just putting her coat on when he walked in. She managed to execute a small start of surprise, carefully schooling her features as she turned to look at him, but pretence was forgotten as she saw the state he was in.

He had paused in the kitchen to remove his boots, but nothing could disguise the fact that he was soaked to the skin. He was shivering visibly and had instinctively moved to the fire, warming his hands in front of it.

'Oliver!' Francesca protested. 'You...'

'Don't fuss,' he told her harshly, and then frowned as he looked at his watch. 'What are you doing here, anyway? You should have left half an hour ago.'

She flinched beneath the accusatory tone of his voice, and although she didn't say anything, he added wearily, 'I'm an adult, Francesca, not a child. I don't want anyone worrying over me like a mother hen, and if I did... I thought we'd already been through this once and disposed of the subject. I don't want your compassion, or your caring, or your pity. In fact, there's only one thing I want from you,' he told her savagely, 'and that's this.'

It came so suddenly, so unexpectedly, like lightning in a clear blue sky, that she was totally unprepared for it. One moment she was standing facing him across the hearth-rug, staring at him in stupefied detachment while his insults fell against her ears, the next she was in his arms, his fingers biting into her skin while his mouth searched for and found her own, and then proceeded to savage it in a kiss that burned her to her very soul, caustic and bitter with fiercely reigned anger that suddenly spilled over his control.

By any rational law that governed human behaviour, she shouldn't have... *couldn't* have responded to him, but, to her own inner disbelief, she found that she *was* responding; perhaps not openly, but definitely and more dangerously, in all the secret places of her heart and body, so that her mouth trembled under his and she was filled with a destructive urge to feed the desire she could feel burning in him until they were both consumed in its flames.

Luckily he seemed to realise their mutual danger before she could do any such thing, releasing her abruptly with a savage sound somewhere between compunction and frustration.

'I'm sorry,' he told her roughly, stepping back from her and raking his hand through his hair to massage the back of his head, something he often did when he was exceptionally tense. 'It's the book...It's getting to me, I'm afraid.'

'Didn't the walk help?' Francesca asked him, careful to keep her back to him while she pretended to rearrange the papers on her desk and fought to recover her composure. She had just been one minute step away from total destruction...or total delight, dependent upon which way one looked at it—and her body, that rebellious and defiant instrument of flesh, was at this precise moment claiming the latter.

'Yes and no. It helped to clear certain problems from my mind, only to give me others. Characters have a way of defying their creator's intentions at times...especially female characters,' he added in a growl.

She had herself under control now, or so she thought, but when she turned to look at him her face was so white that he immediately frowned.

'I'd better run you home. You can't possibly walk. You'll get soaked.'

'There's no need,' Francesca assured him. She wasn't feeling strong enough right now to share the enforced intimacy of a car ride with him, and besides, she could almost feel his impatience to get back to work.

'I'll ring for a taxi.'

Whether or not he would have let her, she had no idea, because at that moment the doorbell pealed, and when Oliver went to answer it he returned with Elliott.

'Beatrice was worried about you walking home in the rain,' he announced as Oliver showed him into the study. 'It seems I've just arrived in time,' he added, and later Francesca wasn't quite sure whether he had meant because she already had her coat on and was on the point of leaving, or whether he had taken one look at her and guessed immediately what had happened.

Although what *had* happened? Oliver had kissed her, that was all... A mere kiss, given more out of the sheer physical and mental frustration of his work than anything else.

There was nothing more to it than that. Only there was... there was a great deal more, like the fact that it had unlocked a door which they had both previously very firmly kept barred and closed, and that now, from her side of that door, Francesca was discovering that something had happened and that it was impossible for her to close it as securely as it had been closed before.

That was *her* problem, she told herself firmly as she prepared for bed. Her problem and hers alone, and she was not going to allow it to affect her relationship with Oliver. It had happened, and now it had to be forgotten.

And she might have succeeded, too, if the second of those fatal three things had not happened.

'But we can't just drop everything and go to New York,' Beatrice was protesting as Francesca walked into the kitchen the next morning.

'Sebastian will never forgive you if we don't,' she heard Elliott warning his wife.

'Oh, I know. But Elliott, how can we go? It would mean taking the children on that long flight... and then we'd have to find somewhere to stay, and then there's Francesca...'

'If we can fly Concorde we can be there in next to no time at all. Accommodation is no problem. In fact, for such a very special occasion, I think it might be an idea if we took Henrietta with us and booked a suite. Knowing you, you'd never have a minute's peace if I suggested leaving the children behind in Henrietta's care. We ought to go, Beatrice... Sebastian needs you to be there.' He saw that Francesca was looking puzzled and explained to her, 'One of Beatrice's twin brothers has been understudying for the male lead in a Broadway play. The lead player has broken his ankle and Sebastian has been asked to take over. It's a major part and a very important opportunity for him. His agent rang us this morning. Sebastian wants us to be there for his opening.'

'Of course you must go,' Francesca agreed, and then she saw the way Beatrice was looking at her, and assured her hostess very firmly, 'Oh, you mustn't worry about me. I assure you that I'm perfectly capable of looking after myself.'

'But it seems so rude. Your grandfather would never approve.'

'I'm twenty-four years old,' Francesca pointed out wryly. 'Please go,' she coaxed Beatrice. 'If you don't, I shall never forgive myself.' And she saw from the quick, approving look Elliott gave her that she had said the right thing.

'Well, if you're sure you don't mind——' Beatrice thanked her. She looked at Elliott. 'I do want to go, it's true, but I feel so guilty dragging the children over there, and you and Henry.'

'Henry will love it, and so will the kids. We'll make time to take them to F.O. Schwartz to see the toys. Stop fussing and start packing while I get on the phone to British Airways.'

Within an hour it was all arranged, and by the time Francesca left the house for work, Beatrice and Henrietta were frantically packing ready for their flight across the Atlantic.

The first thing Francesca noticed when she walked into Oliver's kitchen was how cold it felt, and she soon discovered why. The boiler which heated the water for the central heating system was still out.

She stared at it in dismay and confusion. Oliver was always so insistent upon keeping it going. As she headed for the passage, she saw that Oliver's supper dishes were in the sink.

She missed the scent of freshly brewed coffee which normally greeted her when she walked in to the kitchen, and wondered what Oliver had had for his breakfast.

She knocked briefly on the study door before opening it and walking in, but she needn't have bothered, she discovered, because Oliver wasn't there.

Instead the only occupant of the room was the cat who had adopted Oliver and who normally spent his time curled up in front of the kitchen stove. Now he was almost lying in the hearth, as though desperate to soak up the last warmth of the now dead fire. The curtains were closed; the air in the room heavy with the scent of whisky.

Francesca wrinkled her nose in distaste, her eyes widening as she saw the half-empty bottle standing on Oliver's desk.

Now she knew what it must have felt like to discover the Mary Celeste, Francesca thought whimsically, her illusion that she was alone in the house suddenly destroyed as she heard the sound of a crash from upstairs.

She hurried into the hall and up the stairs without stopping to question what she was doing, pushing open the first door she came to.

Oliver was sprawled out on top of the bed, lying face-down, fully dressed and still apparently fast asleep.

The noise she had heard must have been the lamp which now lay shattered on the floor, and as Oliver moved restlessly she realised that his outflung arm must have caught it.

It seemed impossible that he could have slept through the noise, and her nose wrinkled again as she caught the sweet smell of whisky that pervaded the room. He was breathing loudly, she realised as he rolled over on to his back, the dark growth of overnight beard adding to the already dissolute image presented by his crumpled clothes.

What on earth had prompted him to drink to such an extent? He was normally such an abstemious man. She approached the bed gingerly, a quick frown touching her forehead as she drew closer to him and saw the brilliant flush of colour that burned his cheekbones.

She could almost feel the heat coming off him from where she stood. He coughed in his sleep, a harsh, racking sound that made her own chest feel uncomfortably tight, and then he opened his eyes and focused on her disbelievingly.

'Francesca...'

His voice sounded odd, hoarse and sleep-thickened. The way he said her name, as though unable to credit the fact that she was there, made her heart thump erratically.

'What the——'

He tried to sit up and then fell back against the pillows with a groan, his skin grey where it had been flushed, beads of sweat forming on his upper lip as he fought against the pain even Francesca could see he was suffering.

'Sorry... I must have overslept,' he told her through gritted teeth. 'What time is it?'

'Half-past ten.' He opened his eyes and tried to sit up; a soft groan of pain growled in his throat that made Francesca's stomach muscles tense in sympathy, but she couldn't quite stop herself from glancing at the empty glass on the table beside the bed.

He saw it and said sardonically, 'There's no need to look like that. I didn't spend the night indulging in an excess of alcohol, if that's what you're thinking. I let the boiler go out, and I was so damn cold I thought a nightcap might warm me up.'

'A nightcap?' Francesca queried, remembering the half-empty whisky bottle.

'A nightcap,' Oliver reiterated firmly, starting to move, and then for the first time apparently becoming aware of the fact that he was still fully dressed.

'Hell!' he swore softly. 'I suppose I shouldn't blame you for thinking I'd gone on a bender. My head certainly feels as though it's true. The last thing I can remember is coming up here with the most God-awful headache... I must have practically passed out.'

He was talking more to himself than her, Francesca recognised, accepting that he could only be stating the truth, and feeling her own disquiet increase.

That burning flush was back, and as he tried to stand up he swayed a little, looking down at his own legs as though surprised to discover that they weren't prepared to support him.

He coughed again and then shivered, and, remembering how he had gone out into the storm and the state in which he had returned, Francesca suspected that at the very least he had caught a bad chill.

If that was the case, the very worst thing for him would be the cold dampness of the old house, which was already beginning to seep into her own bones.

'Is there some other means of heating the water, apart from the boiler?' she asked him crisply.

He looked at her vaguely, a sure sign that he could not be feeling well.

'There's an immersion heater.'

'Well, if you tell me where the switch is, I'll turn it on, and then I'll go downstairs and make us both some coffee.'

While she was there she was also going to have an attempt at starting the boiler, she decided grimly, shivering a little herself in the chilly air of the unheated room.

She waited for Oliver to make some objection, to remind her that this was his home and that she was his employee, but a little to her surprise he simply stared at her with glazed eyes and sank back on to his bed with his head in his hands.

'Good God, if I didn't know damn well I only had one drink last night, I'd think I'd sunk the whole bottle. I certainly feel as though I have.'

He shivered violently, his teeth chattering audibly and Francesca wasted no further time.

'The immersion heater?' she reminded him, and when he looked blankly at her, she repeated patiently, 'Oliver, the switch for the immersion heater...so that I can put it on and you can have a hot bath. Where is it?'

'Next to the airing cupboard...next bedroom along,' he told her, adding under his breath as she headed for the door, 'What the hell's wrong with me?'

The muttered question wasn't addressed to her, but Francesca answered it anyway, telling him calmly, 'I think you've caught a chill. And going to bed in those damp clothes can't have helped. You were out in the rain—remember?' she added when he continued to look blankly at her. 'You went for a walk, to clear your thoughts.'

He focused properly on her then, looking not into her eyes but at her mouth, and her whole body burned as she fought to suppress the memory of his kiss.

'Yes...' Oliver said harshly, providing a welcome distraction. 'It's all coming back to me now.' He was still looking at her mouth, but *he* couldn't have been thinking of that kiss, Francesca recognised because he added, 'I worked until about nine o'clock and let the boiler go out... I decided I might as well have an early night and then I had another thought about Bellengaria...something I had to get down on paper.'

'So what time did you stop working?' Francesca asked him.

He shrugged. 'I can't remember. I think it was gone one when I came up here.'

He had worked all that time without anything to eat or drink, and in that cold room. No wonder he had thought that a glass of whisky might warm him up!

'I'll go and put the immersion heater on,' she told him quietly.

She wanted to suggest that it might be a good idea if he stripped off the clothes he was wearing and replaced them with something warmer, but she suddenly felt excruciatingly tongue-tied, as her mind tormented her with far too vivid and intimate mental images of his nude body.

She suddenly felt as though even her presence in his bedroom was an unwarranted intrusion into his privacy, and so she made for the door, pausing only to ask huskily, 'Do you have any extra bedding anywhere, or an electric blanket...something to make you feel a little warmer?'

He focused on her with such brilliant intensity that she could feel the colour rising up under her skin. Of course he wouldn't have an electric blanket. If he ever felt cold in bed, then the only thing he would want to warm him...

Her face grew pink and hot at her own erotic thoughts, and his gaze narrowed dangerously as though he fully intended to read her mind.

He must have done, she realised seconds later as he said softly, 'You're wrong, you know. In actual fact, I prefer sleeping alone.' He turned away from her then, as though he didn't want her to see his face, and added abruptly, 'I think there's a hot-water bottle in one of the drawers in the kitchen, but since I have no intention of going back to bed, I shan't need it.'

Francesca didn't risk arguing with him, hurrying instead into the other bedroom to switch on the immersion heater.

Once downstairs, she found the coffee and set the filter machine in motion.

The kitchen boiler was a modern one, and, she was delighted to discover, relatively easy to clean. Borrowing a pair of Mrs Lyons' household gloves, she completed this task and then went into the small store off the kitchen where she knew the fire-lighters were kept.

The tiny room was icy cold, the damp penetrating right through to her bones, the chill reminding her of her family's home in Venice. That too had the same all-pervading icy dampness, and unlike Oliver's house it did not have the benefit of central heating.

It was because the house did not have gas piped to it that Oliver had to use a solid fuel method of heating the boiler; the house was too far off the beaten track to merit its own private gas supply, so Mrs Lyons had told her.

She poured Oliver a cup of coffee and was just about to take it upstairs to him when he forestalled her by walking into the kitchen.

He was still unshaven, and although he had changed his clothes he didn't look well, Francesca acknowledged as she ignored his scowl.

'You should have left that for me to do,' he said as he saw she had lit the stove.

'And you should have stayed upstairs,' she returned promptly. 'You're not well, Oliver,' she added in a more gentle voice.

'I'm perfectly all right,' he contradicted her flatly, and immediately shivered so violently that he had to grab hold of the table to steady himself.

Francesca very pointedly said nothing, simply gathering up the firelighters and coal she had placed on one side to light the study fire and walking past him.

She heard him coughing as she cleaned and relaid the fire, and her concern deepened. She knew how stubborn men could be about denying they were ill. Her own father had had a bout of pneumonia one winter, thoroughly neglecting himself and ignoring her mother's pleas to him to stay at home and rest.

When she walked back into the kitchen carrying the ashes, she said quietly, 'You aren't well, Oliver, and I really think you should be in bed.'

She didn't look at him as she said it, frightened that her vulnerability might betray her and that she might colour up like an adolescent girl, but for once her self-control did not desert her.

'I've got a deadline to meet—remember?' Oliver reminded her, tight-lipped. 'I've already lost enough time thanks to...'

He was looking at her so bitterly that she automatically took a step backwards, and this time her face did flame, but with shock and not guilty desire. Was he trying to say that she had caused him to lose headway with progress on the book? Was he implying that her research had in some way proved detrimental?

Before she could ask him, he frowned and raked his fingers through his hair, looking both angry and disturbed; looking, she realised, as though he had said something he would have preferred to keep to himself.

'I thought it was Bellengaria who was holding you up,' Francesca commented defensively, knowing that Oliver was experiencing some kind of problem with the female character.

To her chagrin, he ignored her comment and said harshly, 'When you've finished playing at Cinderella, perhaps we could both get down to some work.' And, picking up his coffee, he walked past her into the study.

Arrogant...hateful...horrible man! Francesca stormed as she got rid of the ashes and returned to the kitchen. It would have served him right if she'd just let him lie there and freeze. It came to something when all the thanks she got for trying to be helpful was criticism and contempt...

She picked up her own coffee and headed for the study in a mood of angry defiance. Well, if he wanted to make himself ill by neglecting his health, then let him. And when he *was* ill, *she* wasn't going to lift a finger to help him, she told herself with a great degree of satisfaction.

Only, as the morning wore on and Oliver's harsh, hacking cough grew worse, she found it wasn't quite as easy to distance herself as she had believed.

At half-past twelve, without saying a word to Oliver, she left her work and went into the kitchen to reheat the chicken broth she had made the previous day.

She carried a bowl of it through to him on a tray and put it down in front of him in silence.

She hadn't intended to say anything, but when he looked up at her with hot, glazed eyes that glittered and focused oddly as though he was having difficulty in seeing her, she abandoned her pride and said fiercely, 'I don't care what you say, Oliver. You *are* ill, and I'm going to ring the doctor.'

Later she realised that the mere fact that he only made a token protest was a clear indication of how he must have been feeling, but at the time all she registered was a faint sense of relief that he didn't argue too volubly with her.

She rang Beatrice's doctor who, when she explained the situation, confirmed that it would be quite in order for her to visit Oliver and announced that it sounded to her as though he had picked up a particularly virulent virus that was doing the rounds.

She confirmed this diagnosis an hour later, after she had dealt firmly and, it seemed to Francesca, a little unsympathetically with Oliver's protests that there was nothing wrong with him.

As Francesca showed her out she gave her a wry smile and said, 'I'm afraid it's going to fall on your shoulders to try and make him behave sensibly. I'll make out a prescription for some antibiotics, but I suspect that some time or other in the next twenty-four hours he's going to feel very ill indeed. These things always seem to hit the male sex harder than our own. He's going to be extremely feverish and feel very, very unwell... Would you be able to stay here and keep an eye on him?'

'Do you think I should?' Francesca asked her, trying to ignore the sudden sensation which assailed her stomach of having stepped into an empty lift shaft.

'Well, yes, if you can. He isn't going to be dangerously ill, but I would prefer someone to be with him. Can you stay?'

'Yes,' Francesca told her truthfully.

She didn't say anything about the doctor's request to her when she returned to the study. Oliver was scowling, his head bent over his work, and Francesca diplomatically refrained from saying, I told you so.

By four o'clock he had abandoned any pretence of trying to work and was sitting in a chair in front of the fire, shivering violently.

Francesca, rather than risk an undignified argument, had decided to say nothing to him of her own plans, so at a quarter-past four she calmly gathered together her things and put on her coat.

What she intended to do was to return to Beatrice and Elliott's so that she could collect everything that she would need. She held an international driver's licence and she intended to come back in Beatrice's small car, knowing that her hostess wouldn't mind her using it. She would need to stop in the village for fresh supplies. Mrs Lyons had been called away so suddenly that she hadn't been able to stock up on fresh things.

Also, because it hadn't been decided exactly when Elliott and Beatrice would return, she intended to leave a letter for them explaining what had happened.

In addition to having twin half-brothers in America, both of whom were involved in the production in which Sebastian was to take the leading role, Beatrice's half-sister Lucilla and her husband were in Hollywood on business, and Beatrice had hoped they might be able to fly to New York to join them for the all-important first night.

Francesca, no stranger to the intricacies and intrigues of family life herself, had heard a good deal about Beatrice's younger siblings, although as yet she had not met any of them.

The youngest, William, who was in his last year at Oxford, did apparently spend a good deal of time with Beatrice and Elliott, and so too did Miranda, Beatrice's youngest sister, but she was apparently heavily involved in designing costumes for a fringe theatre group based in Edinburgh and it was not financially viable to make too many expensive train journeys.

Families were odd things, Francesca mused to herself as she let herself into Elliott's home. Beatrice plainly adored hers, even if to judge from Elliott's dry comments he viewed them with a little more distance.

For her own part, while she loved her parents and her brothers dearly, her feelings towards the rest of her family were rather mixed.

She considered her grandfather to be something of a tyrant who enjoyed the power he wielded over the other members of his family. With the benefit of hindsight, she now felt faintly scornful of her old self and her subconscious attempts to placate him with her ready acceptance of his plans for her.

What was it about this plain grey country of her mother's that brought such a refreshing breeze rushing through her life, to remove years of deadening acquiescence and obedience to rules which she was quickly discovering were not necessarily the ones by which she wanted to live her life?

The belief, once so strong in her, that it was her duty to atone for her father's sin in marrying against his father's dictate, had become as distant and amazement-inducing as her childhood belief in magic and fairy-stories; a stage through which she had passed, to emerge into maturity like a caterpillar shedding its chrysalis.

Before her grandfather and Paolo's mother had announced their betrothal, her father had taken her on one side and told her that she must not think that it was his or her mother's wish that the betrothal take place, but she had ignored the escape route he had given her and assured him that she wanted the betrothal.

He had looked far more concerned than a father whose daughter had made such an advantageous betrothal ought to look, she remembered with sudden clarity. And it struck her quite forcibly what a sacrifice her parents had had to make in giving up their independence to return to live under her grandfather's far from benign rule.

The reason for that had been, supposedly, Grandfather's ill health and the necessity of her father taking over the reins of running the family business and estates. As the only son, he had had no other choice, so he had given up the job he had found for himself when he and her grandfather had quarrelled so bitterly when the Duca had discovered that his son fully intended to marry the English girl with whom he had fallen in love.

The Duca had disinherited her father and refused to have him in the house, and now, musing on the recent history of her family, Francesca wondered how often her mother must have wished that it had been possible for them to remain independent.

It had been out of love and concern for her grandfather that they had not, and he had quite callously used that concern against them and against her, she recognised now as she remembered how deliberately and how effectively he had instilled in her as a child the belief she had kept hidden from her parents, that somehow they had let the family down, and that it was up to her as their daughter to atone for their crime.

Yes, her grandfather had a decidedly Machiavellian turn of mind, but she was free of his machinations now. Free to make her own choices ... her own mistakes.

It was almost seven o'clock when she eventually turned into Oliver's drive. She parked Beatrice's car outside the door and then went to open it.

The house was silent, much as it had been this morning, only now it was a good deal warmer. She had checked the stove before she left, and she was relieved to discover that the fire was still going.

She unpacked her shopping first, and then, having brought in her suitcase, made for the study. Oliver opened the door just as she reached it. He seemed to be swaying slightly and his face looked unhealthily flushed, as though he had a high fever.

'What the devil are you doing back?' he demanded savagely as she went towards him.

'The doctor said you weren't to be left alone. She asked if I would stay here and keep an eye on you.'

'Oh, she did, did she? Well, now *I'm* going to tell you that I'm perfectly capable of looking after myself, and that if I did need nannying—which I don't—you . . .'

He seemed to be having trouble focusing on her. His voice faded abruptly and Francesca noted that he had to cling to the doorframe for support.

His obvious weakness concerned her far more than she let him see, and she had to struggle to make her voice sound calm and even as she told him, 'I'm not going to argue with you, Oliver, and neither am I going to leave this house until I'm convinced that you're well enough for me to do so. Now . . . since I can hardly order you to do the sensible thing and go to bed, can I *suggest* that you do so before you collapse completely?'

She suspected that he would have gone on insisting that he was perfectly all right if he hadn't attempted to take a step forward and almost crumpled at her feet.

'All right,' he agreed weakly, leaning against the doorframe. 'You win this time round. Although what the hell you think you're going to prove by playing the ministering angel...'

Francesca flinched beneath the contempt in his voice. 'I'm not trying to prove anything,' she told him quietly.

'That's just as well,' Oliver responded. 'Because, as I've already warned you once—there's no place for a woman like you in my life, Francesca.'

'I agree,' she told him proudly, scarcely allowing herself to recover from the blow of his harsh words, 'and even if there was...I doubt very much that I would want it.'

Just for a second she saw something leap to life in his eyes: a fierce male anger that made her step back from him instinctively as she felt her danger.

Later on, when he was safely in bed, and she was downstairs in the study, she was inclined to be slightly scornful of her rather spineless reaction. What was there to be frightened of, after all? That he would kiss her a second time as he had done the previous evening? She had lived through the experience once and surely must now be fireproof? He had already warned her off once; there had been no need for him to do so a second time, unless, of course, he was aware of what had been happening to her while she worked alongside him...that subtle, pervasive awareness of him that had turned to a sharp, nagging desire, and from that to...to something she wasn't even going to contemplate giving a name, she told herself firmly, and no, of course he wasn't aware of it. How could he be? The man wasn't omniscient. Thank goodness.

CHAPTER SEVEN

ALTHOUGH outwardly she had projected the impression that staying uninvited and unchaperoned at a man's house was something she did every day, inwardly Francesca had been uncomfortably aware of the fact that, in this instance if no other, her grandfather's judgement of the situation would have exactly matched Oliver's; that it was not her business to nursemaid him, and that as a grown man he was perfectly capable of looking after himself.

His virtual collapse at her feet, however, had buoyed up her own wavering conviction that she was doing the right thing, and once he was safely in bed and she had time on her own to consider just what she had done, she found she no longer cared how much her grandfather might have disapproved.

It was the final step forward, she recognised as she sat in Oliver's study, nursing a cup of coffee and almost feeling the chains of duty and obedience snapping and falling away from her as she perceived, not just with her intelligence, but also and more importantly with her heart, that her grandfather was not always right; that there were other ways of living, apart from the way he dictated. She remembered now the look her parents and godparents had exchanged when it had been suggested that she came to England, and with a flash of perception she realised that they *had* been aware of the burden she was carrying, and they had wanted to free her from it.

On impulse she reached for the telephone. She had almost picked up the receiver when she stepped back from it. No; if she rang her parents now a part of her mind might always wonder if she had done so because subconsciously she wanted their support and approval for what she was doing.

She had made her decision and she would stand by it without any support. She would behave like the adult she was.

A wry smile curled her mouth. Wasn't it rather ridiculous that a woman of her age should experience such emotional turmoil, simply because she was staying alone in the home of an unmarried man with whom she had no blood tie?

There was really far too much work to be done for her to sit here dwelling on her own emotions. There was the boiler to be fuelled, for one thing, and a good nourishing broth to be prepared for when Oliver was well enough to eat. She would also have to wake him up later to give him the medication the doctor had told her he was to have at six-hourly intervals.

Fuelling the boiler was a time-consuming but otherwise dull task. However, if she did not want to wake up in the morning and find the house as icy-cold as it had been this morning, it was one that had to be performed, Francesca acknowledged wryly as she brought in the fuel and then adjusted the thermostat so that the stove would stay going overnight.

Making the broth was a far easier task. She had always enjoyed cooking, but now as she worked she missed the rich odours of the *palazzo's* kitchen with its array of dried and fresh herbs and the busy chatter of the maids.

She worked for longer than she had intended, subconsciously putting off the moment, she knew, when she would have to go upstairs and wake Oliver. He wouldn't be pleased to discover that she was still here, and her skin seemed to shrink painfully against her bones as she anticipated his verbal reaction to her defiance.

It wasn't that she feared him—far from it; what she did fear was her own vulnerability to his anger. She was frightened that his rejection of her help would hurt her.

It struck her, as she went upstairs with his medication, that she had fallen into a trap as old as time itself in allowing herself to be physically attracted to a man whom she knew to be just about the worst possible kind of man for her to desire, and if he should discover her folly he would not treat it, or her, gently, she suspected.

She pushed open his bedroom door and walked in quietly. When he had collapsed, she had been more intent on getting him safely upstairs than in paying any attention to his bedroom, but now, with his motionless figure a lean shape beneath the duvet as the light from the landing spilled into the room, she studied her surroundings curiously.

It was a pleasantly large room, with dormer windows; both of them with window-seats and latticed panes. One of them was slightly open, allowing a cool wash of fresh air into the room;

neither of them had the curtains drawn, and she moved quietly to perform this task.

On the bedside chest stood a photograph frame with the same photograph in it as the one downstairs in the study.

How it must have hurt him to lose his child, because in his heart Oliver had considered Katie to be *his* child, Francesca recognised. And the little girl; how had she felt at being wrenched away from the man she knew as her father, to be told that someone else held that role?

No wonder Oliver felt so bitter about his ex-wife and about marriage. She had cheated him in the most cruel way there was; not so much in passing off another man's child as his—many women did that, and many men reared children and loved them without knowing they were not of their blood; the Italian side of Francesca's nature accepted that, in a male-orientated society, women sometimes were forced to such subterfuge. No, Oliver's ex-wife's cruelty had been in allowing him to love her child and then in not just telling him that the child wasn't his, but taking her away from him as well.

She shivered, and stepped back from the window. Any women who was foolish enough to fall in love with Oliver would have a hard time convincing him that that love was real. He had been left dangerously embittered by his ex-wife's cruelty, and, like an animal wounded by a human being it had trusted, he was now ready to savage rather than to risk being hurt again.

And then the third thing happened.

She approached the bed, and as she bent down to wake him up, almost recoiling from the heat coming off his body, he muttered something in his sleep and turned over restlessly.

She had left him to get into bed himself, and as she saw the smooth sleekness of his bare back, she wondered if he merely slept in pyjama bottoms or if perhaps he did not wear anything at all.

Her own thoughts shamed her, bringing a hot sting of guilty colour to her face. She turned away nervously, bumping into the chest as she did so and giving a small cry of pain as she hurt her ankle bone.

She half expected the noise to wake Oliver up, but he still seemed deeply asleep, although he had turned over again, causing the bedclothes to slip further down his body. He was breathing fast, his head turning from side to side in agitation, a frown puckering his forehead. He muttered something that Francesca couldn't hear, and then flung out one arm as though he expected to find someone sleeping next to him.

His chest was shadowed with dark hair that arrowed down to his navel. Francesca drew in a sharp breath and looked away hastily.

She must wake him up and give him his medication. What was she doing standing there and trembling like an aspen just because she had realised that the male body beneath the bedclothes was most probably naked?

Anyone would think . . .

Anyone would think that she was an almost totally inexperienced virgin whose knowledge of a man's body came not from touching it, or knowing it with the intimacy of a lover, but simply from twentieth-century living. . . And this just wasn't *any* man who was making her shiver and ache so disastrously; this was a man who made her feel things she had thought it was impossible for her to experience; this was a man who...

Oliver moved violently, crying out; a low, tormented sound of pain that made her forget her own confusion and reach out instinctively to comfort him, placing her hand on his arm, and bending her head towards him so that her hair brushed silkily against his skin.

He opened his eyes and stared at her, his pupils almost black, surrounded by a silvery iris that seemed to hypnotise her so that she couldn't move, trapped in that silver gleam.

'Garia, you're here... why do you torment me like this?' he demanded thickly.

And Francesca realised instantly that he was rambling... that his fever had taken hold of him, making his dreams so vivid that he believed she was that girl he had himself created out of his own imagination.

She had no idea what to do. Was someone who rambled like a sleepwalker? Would it perhaps be dangerous to try to wake him? Sleepwalkers were supposed to be gently led back to bed and allowed to wake up naturally. If she could just placate him, perhaps she could induce Oliver to go back to sleep and then she would wake him up properly.

She tried to do so, shushing him with soft words, and trying to coax him to lie back against his pillows, but he was too strong for her. He was sitting up now, and she had to avert her gaze from his nude body, so weakening a sensation did the sight of it cause her.

His hands were gripping her wrists, almost painfully tight, as he continued to watch her.

'Why are you tormenting me like this?' he demanded in a low, tortured voice, that shocked her with its raw emotionalism. 'Are you what you seem, my Medici dove?' he went on hoarsely, one hand releasing her wrist, to tangle in her hair and cup the back of her head. 'Or does that sweet face hide a canker that could rot a man's soul; that could destroy a man and send him to hell for all eternity?'

'No...no...' Francesca denied sharply, abruptly falling silent as she realised what she had done, but Oliver's expression had not changed. Her voice had not pierced through his fevered dream at all.

Perhaps it was normal for writers to imagine their characters were real, Francesca reassured herself shakily. For all she knew, Oliver might dream every night about them. Or was it just his fever that had made them feel so real to him that he was confusing her with Bellengaria?

And himself with Kit?

Almost the very second that disturbing thought formed, he pulled her towards him, so unexpectedly that she overbalanced and fell heavily against him.

'You say no,' he told her thickly. 'Soft words drop from your tongue as sweetly as honey. You say you love me and that you want me, and you tell me that you are afraid of your family.

'Come to me now, Garia...prove to me that what you say is the truth.'

Oliver's arms were round her, the fierce drum of his heartbeat thudding against her body. She could feel his tension, his heat ... She *had* to wake him up. But she hesitated for just a fraction of a second too long, and in that brief time-span his mouth found hers and fastened over it, and he kissed her with a need and a hunger that blasted through every defence she had.

She was not a victim of his fever. *She* was not acting out a fantasy created by his illness. She was most certainly not Bellengaria, but none of those things were strong enough to prevent her from being swamped by the wave of feeling that seemed to come from nowhere and roll over her until she could think, feel and breathe nothing other than Oliver.

He was still kissing her, savaging her mouth with the desperate urgency of a desire she had read about but never expected to experience. His tongue probed her lips, and they parted in a willing obedience that shocked her mind. The rough, invasive force of his desire held her in thrall, and by the time she realised exactly what the urgent movement of his tongue mimicked it was too late to deny its possession of the untutored moistness of her mouth.

Heat scalded her, not just at the intimacy she was permitting but at her own responsiveness to it; his hands were on her body, tugging impatiently at her clothes, until the buttons on her shirt opened, leaving him free to caress the fullness of her breasts.

She felt him hesitate as though her bra was something unexpected and unfamiliar; as no doubt it would have been to a man from the sixteenth century, she realised as she wondered frantically what on earth she ought to do.

To wake him now would be to expose herself to embarrassment and humiliation—and to his knowledge as well as her own that she had done nothing to wake him before. No. Better to ease herself away from him and then to wake him. But what if he would not let her go? What if...

She cried out softly in alarm as his hands found the catch on her bra and released it. She must stop him. She must stop him now before things went any further. But the heat of his flesh against her own, the raw, satisfied sound of pleasure he made as he pressed the delicate coolness of her naked breasts into the heat of his own flesh, destroyed her will-power.

His hands tangled in her hair as he kissed her jaw and her throat, hot, fierce kisses that burned her skin, interspersed with slurred, and sometimes shocking phrases that sent her mind as out of control as her body.

He *was* naked, she realised numbly as the bed-clothes slipped away and he drew her urgently against him. He was naked and he was aroused, and he believed she was a woman who did not and never could exist... and if she did not stop him he would take her and possess her as though she *were* that woman. She *had* to stop him.

His mouth had reached her shoulder-blade; soon she would feel its moist heat on her breast; soon he would kiss her... touch her in a way that no one ever had, and she wanted that fierce tug of his mouth against her flesh, she realised achingly. She wanted him to take her and love her and drown them both in that fierce tide of need she could feel surging through him.

But she couldn't allow herself to give in to such feelings...

Achingly, she lifted her hands to his face. 'No...
I must go...'

He tensed and stopped kissing her.

'I must go,' she repeated, and then, taking advantage of his momentary relaxation, she eased herself away from him, and from his bed. Her fingers trembled as she dressed herself, not daring to take her eyes off the figure on the bed.

He called after her once as she left him, and the sound of it tore at her heart. She felt like the worst kind of traitor, and it made no difference knowing that his desire was for a fictional woman who simply did not exist.

He was still asleep...still very restless...and she prayed that when he did wake up, if he remembered anything, he would remember it only as a dream. She was tempted to simply leave his room without trying to wake him, but there was his medication.

Still trembling inwardly, she walked up to the bed and switched on the beside-lamp, firmly gripping his shoulder and shaking him as she did.

He woke up instantly and focused on her with a frown. 'What the...?'

He moved to sit up, and Francesca saw his eyes widen slightly and the feverish colour deepen along his cheekbones as he tensed momentarily.

Instinctively she knew it was his physical arousal that had checked him, and she fought back her own hot tide of guilty colour. If she blushed now...but thankfully she did not.

'It's time for your medication,' she told him as calmly as she could. 'I'm sorry to waken you, but the doctor did say you were to take it every six hours.'

'I thought I told you to leave.'

Francesca felt weak with relief. If he remembered anything at all, he plainly did not connect his dream with her.

'Your doctor told me to stay. Here ... take these, please.'

She handed him the antibiotics and a glass of water.

'I'm staying here until your doctor says I can leave,' she told him firmly, and then added with what she knew to be dangerously provocative mockery, 'If you're worried about your reputation ...'

He looked at her, a hard direct look that made her want to flinch, but she held her ground.

A shiver convulsed him, distracting his attention. He looked both angry and surprised, as though unused to the claims that illness could make on the human body. No doubt he was not pleased to discover that he was as human as everyone else, Francesca thought wryly, as she stepped back from the bed and switched off the lamp.

She dared not linger; she didn't want to tempt fate, or his memory, too far.

'I shan't need to disturb you again until the morning,' she told him as she headed for the door. 'I'm sorry I had to wake you up.'

He made no attempt to detain her, and she breathed a shaky sigh of relief once she was outside his bedroom door.

Now, when she was safely removed from the potency of his presence, she was stunned by the way she had behaved. How could she have allowed herself...? Biting hard on her bottom lip, she hurried down the corridor in search of a spare bedroom as far away from Oliver's as it was possible to get.

Once in bed, she couldn't sleep. The memory of the way she had felt when he kissed her wouldn't let her. To go to sleep would be to escape from facing up to the truth, and she couldn't allow herself to do that.

When had she started to love him? And how had it happened without her even being aware of her own danger? True, she had known that she was *attracted* to him, but she had put that attraction down to the fact that he was different from any other man she had known, that they were working closely together...that he obviously found her physically desirable, a sure balm to any woman's feminine pride, especially when it had been dented as hers had been. She might not have loved Paolo, but she *had* been prepared to marry him and it had hurt when he had rejected her. She had begun to question her own femininity...to wonder if there was something about her that made her unattractive to the male sex. And then Oliver had looked at her, had given her that comprehensive all-male look that had told her plainly that there was nothing wrong with her at all. But he had given her no encouragement to fall in love with him...none at all.

So why had she done so? Not because she was the sort of woman who at all costs had to fall in love and marry. Falling in love with Oliver was the last problem she needed to give herself right now.

He didn't return her feelings, she knew that. But he wanted her.

How dangerous a temptation that knowledge was, whispering to her that although she might not be able to share a lifetime of sharing and growing together with him, of being a part of his life and his work, of having his children, then at least she could have the sharp, almost bitter pleasure of knowing him as a lover.

Only tonight she had discovered what a very sensual man he was.

By his own admission it had been a long time since a woman had shared his life... his bed. With a little gentle encouragement, might he not give way to the desire she had felt flaring between them at odd moments?

Her own thoughts shamed her, causing her face to burn even though she was alone in her room. Had she really changed so much that she was willing to physically seduce a man she knew quite well would never return the depth of her emotional commitment to him, merely for the physical pleasure of having him make love to her?

Yes, she had changed. Or perhaps she had never really known herself at all. Perhaps her responsiveness, like so many other aspects of her personality, had been something she had suppressed and controlled so that she could more readily fit into her grandfather's image of her.

It was a disquieting thought. She sat up in bed and linked her arms around her knees. It was like turning a corner and coming face to face with an abrupt and unexpected mirror image of oneself...recognisable and yet shockingly different, thus exposed so unexpectedly.

She was half afraid of this previously unknown Francesca, she admitted...half frightened by her and half envious of her, that she could so easily contemplate something that her old familiar self would never have dared to even dream of doing, never mind actually consider putting into action.

But old habits die hard, and Francesca knew that, much as she might long to have the mental and emotional daring to openly seduce Oliver into being her lover, she knew that she wouldn't...couldn't...

And yet if tomorrow he should look at her and remember tonight...remember how he had touched her and held her...remember... Her stomach tensed, her body starting to tremble inwardly with longing and fear.

If he should look at her and want her... If he should let her see that he desired her, she knew she would go to him, she acknowledged with a shiver.

It was in the hands of fate to decide, the onus of any action taken from her.

It was as though, in touching her tonight, he had stripped from her all her protective defences, leaving her unable to hide herself from the truth any longer. He had kissed and desired her as a woman who was only a creature of his own imagination, but *she* had responded to him as some part of her had always known she one day must to the man she loved.

She had been completely powerless to prevent her own response, completely lost in the shock of her own desire, her discovery that the ache inside her came not merely from sexual need but from something more; something she had fought against admitting to feeling almost from the first moment she saw him.

She shivered again and sank down beneath the bedclothes. In the morning, would he remember what had happened? Would he look at her and remember that he had confused her with Bellengaria? Would he...

Her mind, exhausted by the trauma of the day, refused to support any more thoughts. Her eyes closed and she slept, but not restfully.

CHAPTER EIGHT

FRANCESCA woke up abruptly, as though someone close at hand had called her name, but as she lay tensely in her bed, listening to catch any trace of the sound that might have woken her, she heard nothing.

She shivered a little as she got out of bed, not wanting to admit that the voice that had roused her from her sleep and whose echoes still rang across her mind had been Oliver's. She had been dreaming that they were in Italy together... that she had run from him and he had pursued her. He had called after her, a harsh, despairing cry, the tone of his voice that in which he had cried out the name of his fictional heroine the previous night.

She showered and dressed in the unused bathroom opposite her purloined bedroom, reflecting that the upstairs of the house badly needed a woman's warming touch. Both Oliver's bedroom and this one were adequately furnished, but they lacked the warmth and little comforts that would have made them far more welcoming.

It was a good, solid house, just the right size for a small family, and she could understand why Oliver had bought it. With its solid stone walls and ancient beams, it breathed security and protection. It was easy to imagine him taking refuge here after the deaths of his ex-wife and her child.

Her Italian heritage rose up within her and she stopped what she was doing, wishing with all the fierce passion of her blood that *she* could give him children; not to obliterate from his memory that other child, but so that he might once again have someone on whom to lavish the love he had given that child. It was wrong that a man who so obviously enjoyed being a father should deliberately choose to shut all that emotion away. He had been badly hurt by his marriage and now he was trying to protect himself, and she must stop indulging in stupid daydreams, she told herself drily as she finished dressing.

As she walked towards the top of the stairs, she hesitated outside his door. There was no sound from inside, but she couldn't help giving in to the temptation to open the door and go in.

Oliver was lying on his stomach, one arm flung out across the bed, his dark hair tousled. His sleep was much more relaxed than it had been the previous night. She hesitated for a moment and then froze as he turned his head and opened his eyes. Shock narrowed them to silver slits.

'What time is it?' he demanded abruptly, starting to sit up. Remembering his nudity, Francesca hastily averted her head, but either deliberately or by a lucky accident he had manoeuvred the quilt so that only the upper half of his chest was exposed as he sat up.

'I don't know... My watch is still in my room.'

'Your room... You mean you stayed here last night?'

It was obvious from his expression that not only didn't he remember mistaking her for Bellengaria, if indeed he remembered such a dream at all, but neither did he remember collapsing and being helped to bed by her, nor being woken up in the night so that she could give him his medication.

Francesca took a deep breath, allowing the relief to seep slowly through her. She hadn't wanted him to remember the reckless way she had responded to him, or to guess from that response what she herself had come to know. For her pride's sake, she didn't want him to know that it was anything more than mere desire she felt for him. He had warned her from the first that love was an emotion that had no place in his life. Even now she could still hear his words ringing through her mind.

Her desire for him was different; that was something she need not hide, because he experienced it himself, she was sure; but her love... That was a secret she would have to keep, and, forcing herself to appear calmly normal, she went through the events of the previous evening, beginning with his collapse.

'In fact, you're due for another dose of medication now,' she warned him, watching him tensely, waiting to see in his eyes that her reference to having to wake him the previous night to administer the drugs prescribed by his doctor had activated his memory.

It obviously hadn't. For him, what had happened, if he recalled it at all, would be merely part of a fevered dream when his characters had turned into real-life people.

As Kit, he had called out to Bellengaria with such longing and hopelessness... Almost as though he loved her... She shivered. Was that possible? For someone to fall in love with a fictional character they had created themselves? He had sounded almost tortured when he spoke to her. No, *not* to her, she reminded herself—not to her, but to Bellengaria.

'I'll get your tablets,' she told him huskily.

It was too late now to wish she had had the vision to see forward into the future that first time she had met him. The damage was done. She loved him.

Oliver insisted that he was going to get up and work, despite Francesca's protests.

He did manage to get himself dressed and down-stairs, but Francesca suspected it was pride alone that kept him sitting at his desk, his head bent over his work.

He was now deep in the most vital section of the book. Kit was in France and had met Bellengaria, and the two of them were now playing out their roles against the glittering background of the medieval court.

Oliver hadn't offered to let her read the new chapters, and she hadn't dared ask, but she knew from the research details he had asked her for where he was up to.

She watched him hungrily, her mind absorbing and storing up every tiny piece of information it could, greedily eager to preserve as many memories as possible. Her time with him was running out. Once the book was finished he would not need her.

He flung a curt question at her without lifting his head, and it took her several seconds to dis-sociate herself from her inward private yearnings and concentrate on clarifying the point he had raised, and in those few vital seconds he raised his head and looked at her.

It was as though they were communicating on two very separate levels, Francesca acknowledged, a tiny tremor of intense awareness gripping her as he looked at her. Desire flared briefly in his eyes, swiftly checked and replaced by a hard anger. He didn't want to want her. She sympathised with him.

'I don't think it would be a good idea for you to stay here a second night,' he told her abruptly, betraying the fact that his concentration on his work was wandering as much as her own.

'I promised the doctor I would,' Francesca told him quietly.

'And I absolve you from that promise,' was his harshly uncompromising response.

She looked gravely at him, and he looked away.

'Why don't you want me to stay?' she asked him quietly, her heart pounding in frantic, heady agitation. Why had she challenged him like that? What if he told her that he had guessed how she felt and that...

'Don't be naïve,' his harsh voice cut through her runaway thoughts. 'You aren't a fool, Francesca, so don't start trying to pretend that you are. 'What did Beatrice say when you told her you were staying here?' he asked her abruptly.

Francesca bit her lip. She couldn't lie to him. She looked directly at him and said quietly, 'She doesn't know. She and Elliott are in New York.'

There was a brief pause. He got up and walked over to the window, standing staring out, with his back to her. His voice was slightly muffled when he did speak and she had to strain to hear all that he was saying. She took a step towards him and then tensed, aching to close the distance between them, and yet all too well aware that Oliver had put that distance there deliberately.

'Do you think, if Beatrice had known, that she wouldn't have counselled you to think again?' he asked her. 'Beatrice knows the kind of man I am, Francesca.'

'Meaning that I don't? Well, then, perhaps you'd better tell me what kind of man you are.'

'Do I really have to?' He swung round, his eyes glittering with a heat that had nothing to do with his fever. Francesca's heart jumped into her throat as he studied her with openly sensual appraisal, her flesh responding instinctively to the intoxicating lure of his desire.

'Very well, then, I shall,' he grated at her. 'I'm the kind of man who finds it damn near impossible to work with a beautiful woman without wondering what it would be like to take her to bed.

'I'm talking about physical desire here, Francesca, and nothing else. An ache...an itch...a need to be satisfied without any kind of emotional, or lasting commitment.'

He saw her face go white, but he wouldn't stop.

'I see I'm beginning to get through to you at last...that ivory tower you inhabit won't always protect you, you know. That cool, virginal air you carry around with you like an invisible shield just begs to be destroyed, did you know that?'

He was angry. Lividly, furiously angry, as much with himself for desiring her, she suspected, as with her for being desirable.

'It takes two to make love,' she told him shakily
when she saw that he was waiting for her response.

It was plainly the wrong one to give. He came
towards her, and for a moment she thought he intended to take hold of her and shake her. He actually reached out towards her, but then let his
hands fall back to his sides, his jaw compressing as
he fought to control the urge to take hold of her.

'You haven't listened to a word I've said, have
you?' he challenged acidly. 'I'm not talking about
making love, Francesca. I'm talking about sex. I'm
talking about a hunger that eats into you and de-
vours you...an ache that has nothing
tender...nothing caring...nothing loving whatsoever about it.'

He broke off his impassioned speech with an impatient sigh, pushing his fingers through his already
untidy hair.

'Oh, hell!' he swore, turning his back on her.
'Can't you see how explosive a situation we have
here?' He swung back towards her, a febrile glitter
darkening his eyes. 'Do I have to spell it out for
you, Francesca?'

He saw the stubbornness in her face and
grimaced.

'All right then, I will, but don't blame me if you
don't like what you hear,' he warned her. 'There
are times, increasingly frequent times, when your
presence here in my home, in this room, arouses
me to the point where I can hardly think of anything other than my need to possess you. So far
I've managed to control that need, but I can't
guarantee that I'm always going to be able to do
so.' He looked at her and asked quietly, 'Now tell

me, what do you think your grandfather would say if he knew you were staying here alone with me?'

Her expression almost gave her away, but she was a lot wiser now than she had been only weeks ago. What she was fighting for here was more than just her independence. She was fighting for her right to make her own decisions...to choose for herself what her life would be, and with whom she would share it and why. She was almost tempted to say to him that perhaps the easiest way around the problem was for him to take her to bed...another woman, a more sophisticated and experienced woman could perhaps have made it, but she wasn't sure that she would be able to carry the suggestion off with the calm detachment it required, especially if he should choose to ask her exactly what she would have to gain from taking him as her lover. She wasn't sure she would be able to lie convincingly enough to hide the truth from him, and she sensed now, after what he had just told her, that he would put the entire breadth of the earth between them if he suspected for one moment how she felt about him.

'My grandfather is not me,' she told him coolly, struggling to heed the inner voice that told her to be cautious and tread carefully, and not give in to her own aching desire to throw away pride and wisdom and take what the moment offered. That would be the action of a heedless child, and after the sweetness of their intimacy would come the burden of self-revulsion. Not because they had made love, but because she would have deceived both herself and Oliver about her feelings for him. 'I make my own decisions about my life, but you're

right: to share the act of sex with a man simply out
of curiosity and desire is not for me. I may not be
experienced, but at least I have the wisdom to know
that much. Will you want me to work for you until
you've finished the book, or would you prefer me
to leave immediately?'

She saw that she had taken him by surprise. What
had he expected? she wondered, the pride she had
not felt before suddenly surging up inside her,
making her hold herself together and not give in to
the pain hammering through her.

'If I had any sense at all I would tell you to go
now,' Oliver told her grimly. 'But I can't finish the
damned book without you, and if I don't...'

It wasn't her task to make his burdens easier to
bear, Francesca reflected, but all her life she had
watched her sex smoothing and easing the pathways
of the men in their lives, and some instincts were
impossible to suppress, so she said calmly, 'Perhaps
now that we are both aware of the...dangers...they
will prove easier to bear.' She gave him a direct look
and prayed that she would sound convincing as she
added firmly, 'You don't strike me as a man who
would force any woman sexually, Oliver, and since
I can promise you that I have no intention of having
a sexual relationship with you...'

'Even though you desire me,' he interrupted,
completely confounding her.

She tried to look away from him and found that
she couldn't. He wasn't making this easy for her,
damn him, and that sudden surge of anger that he
should, manlike, put the onus of controlling his
desire on her shoulders, and then, when she tried
to do so, attempt to undermine her so carelessly,

bolstered her determination and she was able to say quietly, 'Yes . . . even though I desire you. You see, for me, desire, no matter how intense or immediate, could never be enough.'

To her astonishment, instead of the contempt she had expected, she saw something almost approaching respect lighten his gaze.

She was starting to shake, she realised, and she was powerless to stop doing so. She reached out to steady herself by leaning her hand on the back of a chair. She felt oddly dizzy and light-headed. It was an effort to concentrate on what Oliver was saying to her; she felt as though her body had suddenly been left weak by the effort of not betraying to him how she felt, and now all her strength was gone.

'Yes . . . for you commitment would always be important. Once I shared those ideals . . . a lifetime ago, it seems now; and it might be sentimental of me, but I don't think I want to be the one to destroy yours and to show you how unimportant even the strongest ideals are when they try to withstand the full force of the human sexual drive. It cost you a great deal to say what you just did,' he told her, shattering her fragile composure with his perception. 'I'll try to be correspondingly honest with you.

'This book's giving me hell. None of the characters are behaving as they should. Bellengaria, in particular. I intended her to be a powerful pawn on the side of the Medicis . . . a soft, docile creature outwardly, but inwardly as corrupt as the rest of the clan. Kit has endured the trauma of loving someone once. He doesn't need to go through that again. I wanted him to use her and then discard her to her fate...a fate she thoroughly deserved. The Medicis do not show mercy for failure...not even to their own.'

As he talked, Francesca sensed that he was talking more to himself than to her...that it was for his own benefit that he confided his confusion that his plot had apparently changed direction. She sensed with a woman in love's intuition that it was his ex-wife on whom he had based his character...that it was her betrayal of him that he was working through in giving her faults to Bellengaria, and that Kit was in many ways himself. A man who had endured great pain and who had lived through it, like someone burned by fire and now armoured against it.

And last night...that tormented need she had heard in his voice when he called out Bellengaria's name...had that been because deep in his heart he still loved his ex-wife, or simply because in his dream as Kit he had been racked by his desire for a woman who belonged with his enemies and who could betray him?

Francesca had no way of finding out.

He turned to her and said fiercely, 'I can't let you go. I need you too much.' And then, as though the words had shocked him as much as they had her, he focused on her in confusion mixed with anger as he added in a calmer tone, 'I can't finish the book without you, and so if you're really fool enough to stay despite my warning, I'm afraid I'm going to be too selfish to send you away.'

Had they been for her or for Bellengaria, those passionate words of compulsive need? She rather suspected the latter, but that didn't stop her from feeling a dangerously heady sense of joy sweep through her. He needed her... he was asking her to stay.

It wasn't until later that she realised he was also placing on her too vulnerable shoulders the burden of controlling their mutual desire.

He was as human as any other man, she recognised, and it cheered her up in an odd way to know this... to know that, despite his formidable armouring, he wasn't entirely invulnerable.

They worked late into the afternoon. Oliver seemed to be possessed by a powerful surge of energy and drive, and she wondered if it had perhaps been released by the drama of the morning.

She, in contrast, felt drained and on edge. She found it difficult to concentrate on her work, especially when Oliver continued to bombard her with questions, minute details of facts covering such a wide range of topics that she was exhausted by the time four o'clock came.

Normally this was when they stopped work, and she closed her notebook when she heard the clock strike the hour. Oliver must have seen the movement even though she had thought he was concentrating on his writing. He stopped typing and looked across at her.

'When are Beatrice and Elliott expected back from the States?'

'I don't know,' she admitted. 'It was a last-minute decision. Apparently one of the twins has been asked to step into the main lead role in a Broadway play, and of course they wanted to go and see him...'

'You mean Beatrice did, and Elliott, because he adores her, no matter how well he tries to conceal it, gave in and agreed to take her.'

'I think the decision was by mutual consent,' Francesca argued mildly.

'So there's no one in the house,' Oliver persisted.

'No, Henrietta went with them to look after the children,' Francesca agreed with a frown, not sure where his questioning was leading.

'Then you probably had better spend the night here,' he told her, on a sigh of resignation, stunning her.

'But . . .'

'You'll be quite safe,' he assured her curtly. 'I intend to work through the night . . . or for as long as I can. I might as well make the most of it while the mood's on me.'

'But you can't do that,' Francesca protested. 'You're not well enough. You shouldn't have been working today!'

'Because of a mild fever?' he scoffed. 'Don't be ridiculous. Look, I'm not pushing you to stay. You can leave if you wish. I just thought it might be safer for you to stay here than in an empty house. I give you my word I'm not making plans to assault your virginity, if that's what's worrying you.'

'It isn't,' Francesca denied, flushing angrily at the sarcasm in his voice. 'If I'm worried about anything, it's your idiotic lack of regard for your health.'

She didn't realise how severe she sounded, and was puzzled by the amusement that flashed like silver lightning through his eyes until he explained, 'You can be disconcertingly un-Italian at times,

Francesca...very, very English and down-to-earth, in fact. Your late fiancé did you a favour, you know. You would never have been happy playing the role of an obedient Italian wife. The intimacy of an unhappy marriage can be one of the cruellest burdens life gives us to bear.'

'Was your marriage like that?' Francesca asked him quietly.

She thought for a moment he intended to ignore her, but then his frown lightened and he said quietly. 'My marriage was a mistake from the beginning. It should never have happened. I made the classic mistake of confusing passion with love. By the time I realised that all that I felt for Kristie was physical desire and that all she felt for me was that I was a convenient fool she could use to hide her affair, it was too late. We were married.

'My own parents' marriage lasted for over forty years. They were good friends as well as lovers. I was their only child and superfluous to their lives, really. I was born when my mother was forty-two, an unexpected and, I suspect, rather unnecessary addition to their lives.

'In my naïveté, I assumed that my marriage would be like theirs. You see, those of us who have not witnessed at first hand the complications, the traumas, the pains of an adult relationship that goes wrong, are at a considerable disadvantage when we grow up. We expect our lives to mirror those of our parents. We expect to marry and be content. As I said, I was very naïve when I married.'

'Your parents...' Francesca began, fascinated by this unexpected door he had opened for her, this glimpse into his life when she had never expected to be permitted. It was like stepping from the cold of winter through into the warmth of summer, and she basked in the pleasure of it as she waited for his response.

'Dead now, both of them. My father from a heart attack and my mother, I suspect, simply because she could not bear to be apart from him. She was a very formidable woman, my mother, and I think she simply willed herself to die.'

He saw the shocked compassion in her face and said coolly, 'Don't pity me...it's not necessary. As I've already said, I grew up knowing that my place was not at the heart of their lives. They had each other, and for them that was enough.'

They had excluded him from their mutual love and that had hurt him, Francesca recognised, and with a flash of perception she realised how he must have suffered at the loss of the little girl he had thought of as his child. He must have lavished on her all the love he could not give his wife...all the love he himself had been denied as a child.

She lowered her head so that he couldn't see what was in her eyes, but he had already turned his attention back to his work and was totally engrossed in it. So much so, in fact, that she doubted he was even aware of her getting up and leaving the room.

It was time for his medication, and she was hungry and thirsty. She walked into the kitchen and opened the fridge. If she was going to stay the night, after all, she might as well start preparing a meal.

As she opened the fridge door she had a vivid and unnerving mental image of him as he had been last night, reaching for her...needing her. Her hand shook and she almost dropped the milk bottle she was holding.

If he should come to her tonight...if he should... But he wouldn't, and even if he did she wasn't going to let him make love to her when he had told her so plainly and so brutally just why he might want to possess her.

She supposed she should thank him for that. At least he was being honest with her. Another man might not have been so brutally frank, might have taken advantage of her inexperience and very obvious desire for him and let her think that there could be some emotional bond between them simply to satisfy his own sexual need. But that would never be Oliver's way, she recognised. Brutal he might be, but honesty would always be of prime importance to him. Had she been more experienced, she suspected that they would by now be lovers, and yet, oddly, she didn't regret her ignorance. It gave her a deep inner well of pleasure to know that if he did ever come to her, he would be her first lover. She wanted it to happen; she wanted to share with him all the mysteries...all the pleasures...but not on the terms he had outlined so plainly to her earlier.

She only prayed that her will was strong enough to support her deeply held belief that she could only share her body with a man with whom she had a deep emotional bond.

The cat coming in from outside and winding itself round her ankles as it purred loudly brought her back to reality and the mundane pain of hunger grumbling in her stomach.

CHAPTER NINE

PERHAPS because of her lack of sleep the previous night, Francesca slept surprisingly well. She woke up early and from such a deep sleep that for several seconds she had difficulty in remembering where she was, but she *had* known the second she opened her eyes exactly how she felt about Oliver.

She wondered how late he had worked, and, once dressed, walked quietly past his bedroom door, ignoring the temptation to linger there, telling herself that after his late night he would not appreciate being woken up.

Downstairs she checked the boiler and restoked it, fed the cat, made herself some coffee and prepared some breakfast for herself: fresh orange juice from the fruit she had bought in the village and two pieces of wholemeal toast. She was not a breakfast person, but acknowledged the wisdom that healthy living involved at least making a token gesture towards recognising such a meal.

It was only after she had done all this that she headed for the study. The fire would need cleaning out and relighting. Trust a man to resist all attempts to replace this inconvenience with something much cleaner and far less time-consuming, when he was not the one who had the repetitious job of attending to it every winter morning, she reflected.

On the other hand, in the late afternoon when dusk fell and the wind sent the bare branches of the wistaria scratching against the window-panes, there was something undeniably comforting about the warmth of those burning coals which could not really be matched by artificial coals or logs, no matter how skilfully they were manufactured.

She was just acknowledging this as she pushed the study door open.

The shock of seeing Oliver slumped behind his desk, his head pillowed on the papers scattered on it as he lay deeply asleep, held her immobile for several seconds. How late had he worked, totally exhausting himself, to have fallen asleep like that?

He couldn't possibly be comfortable. He was bound to wake up with a stiff neck and a sore back. Francesca walked determinedly across to him, and reached out to shake him awake.

He had stripped off his sweater, and as her fingers curled round his arm she felt the hardness of the muscles beneath the fine wool shirt. A slow curl of sensation began to slide through her stomach. Her hand trembled slightly, and she was conscious of an insanely dangerous desire to allow her fingers to slide caressingly down the length of his forearm. Her heart started to beat too fast, a hot surge of colour storming her face. Yesterday she had been so convinced that she had the strength of will to withstand his physical need of her, and yet here she was this morning, aching to reach out and touch him.

Her fingers trembled lightly against his arm. Her mouth was trembling as well, she recognised, as she bit down hard on her bottom lip in an effort to control it. In fact her whole body felt as though it was gripped by an unfamiliar fever that burned her in waves of body-tensing heat.

Mindlessly she allowed her fingers to smooth the soft fabric of his shirt, acutely aware of the fine, silky hair beneath the cloth; tracing the powerful line of muscle and bone; lost in a forbidden dream of what it would be like to touch her lips to his skin; to absorb the heat and scent of him, to...

'Garia... you're here.'

The slurred, sleepy words jerked her back to reality, and she snatched her hand away, upsetting a pile of books as she did so. They crashed on to the floor, making what, to her over-sensitive ears, sounded like a preternaturally loud noise.

Oliver was awake instantly, frowning at her as he struggled to sit up, only the wary shadow in his eyes betraying his realisation of what he had said.

'Sorry about that,' he said harshly, straightening up from the desk and wincing slightly as he moved his neck. 'It's this damned book. Nothing is turning out the way I'd planned, and it's *your* fault,' he told Francesca, causing her to flush slightly at the curt criticism.

'I'm sorry if my research isn't of a high enough standard,' she began, but he cut through her stilted speech and told her angrily,

'It isn't your research, damn you, Francesca, it's *you*. It's because of *you* that nothing's going the way it should! That my characters...' He broke off abruptly, his mouth hardening as though he already regretted what he had said. 'I'm going to bed for a couple of hours,' he told her. 'I'm as tired

as hell. Wake me up in two hours, will you, please?
I've still got a lot to get through today.'

Francesca watched him go in silence. Her throat
was choked with a mixture of anger, pain and
shock. She had thought for a moment that he was
criticising her research, and instead he had totally
destroyed her illusion that they were working well
together by telling her that *she* was responsible for
the fact that the book was not going well. Why?
Because she disturbed his concentration...
because he desired her.

Without really knowing how she got there, she
found herself standing behind Oliver's desk. She
bent automatically to pick up the books he had
knocked over, and then started tidying up the scattered sheets of typed paper, but all the time she
knew she was only delaying the implementation of
a decision she had already made.

Like a sleepwalker, she sat down at the desk, and
then, feeling almost as deceitful as a person reading
a very personal and private diary without the
owner's consent, she started to read.

The early chapters which she had already read
dealt almost exclusively with Kit's refusal to do as
Sir Francis Walsingham wished and work for him
as he had done before his marriage.

Those chapters had contained vivid and moving
descriptions of Faversham Court and the life Kit
and Rosemary lived there away from court while
Rosemary awaited the birth of their first child.

And then the unexpected and brutal attack on
the house in Kit's absence and the murder of
Rosemary and their child. Kit's grief and anger followed, and then his discovery that his wife and son

had been murdered by members of a secret Catholic sect dedicated to restoring a Catholic monarch to the English throne; a plot which was said to have its origins within the powerful Medici family.

Between them Walsingham and the Queen managed to persuade Kit that he owed it to his wife to avenge her death and, since Faversham Court now tormented him with its memories, he had given in and returned to his old life as a spy.

Walsingham had decided that, in order to make it possible for Kit to infiltrate the Medici family and to discover the names of those in England who were sympathetic to the Catholic cause and who supported it financially and were thus traitors to their Queen, Kit was to pretend that he blamed Walsingham and the Queen for his wife's death, that he was convinced that they had had her and their child murdered in order to get him to return to spying, and that because of this he had now turned his back completely on his Queen and in a gesture of bitterness and revenge was prepared to offer his services to the Catholic faction.

Francesca knew that it had been Oliver's intention that Kit should discover the information he needed through his relationship with Bellengaria and that Bellengaria should always remain a shadowy figure, whose emotions were shallow and whose loyalties could be claimed by any man prepared to admire and flatter her, but, as Francesca discovered as she read what Oliver had written, Bellengaria had developed a much more positive character and taken on a much more important role.

Her relationship with Kit, which was to have been no more than the cynical determination of a man who intended to use her vanity to help him to discover the murderers of his wife, had become intensely emotional and passionate, with neither of them able to trust the other and with both of them caught in the desire that flared so unexpectedly between them.

Bellengaria, orphaned young and brought up in the Medici household, had learned as a child to guard not only her words, but also her thoughts. She had also seen at first hand the cruelty and vice of which her Medici relations were capable, and had learned from it to be very wary and cautious about whom she gave her trust and affections to; so much so that Kit, who had expected to seduce her into being his pawn, had quickly found that, while she responded to his flattery and charm with a smile of apparent acquiescence, she remained stubbornly aloof from any real intimacy. And would have continued to do so if Kit had not found her comforting one of the maids who had been a victim of Cesare's lust; it had been in protecting the young girl that she had betrayed to Kit her true nature with its fierce passions and beliefs.

Caught up in the story, at first Francesca didn't recognise in the conflict between Bellengaria and Kit the similar conflict that existed between Oliver and herself; didn't realise that Kit's discovery that the real Bellengaria was as different from the image she projected as it was possible for a woman to be, mirrored Oliver's own reaction to her... that, in writing so vividly about the passion and emotions which flared between them in a way that neither of them welcomed, Oliver was trying to work through his own desire for her.

When she did, the shock of that recognition made her drop the typed sheet she was reading and sit trembling, her throat tight and sore with suppressed tears, caused by Oliver's almost too painful description of how, after succumbing to his desire for Bellengaria, he had been forced to reject her in order to save both their lives.

She read the last chapter a second time, feeling her own flesh react disturbingly to the passion Oliver had generated between his two main characters.

The hall clock in the hall chimed the hour and she looked up abruptly, appalled to realise that it was over three hours since Oliver had gone upstairs.

Wake me in two hours, he had told her... She got up clumsily and hurried into the kitchen, quickly making some fresh coffee. He would be furious with her, and rightly so.

She was just about to knock on his bedroom door when he stepped out of the bathroom opposite it, a towel wrapped round his lower body, his skin still slightly damp and glowing from his shower.

She knew she ought to move to one side to let him walk into his bedroom, but it was as though her feet were glued to the carpet. She simply could *not* move, nor avert her gaze from absorbing every tiny detail of his bare torso.

'I'm sorry I didn't wake you,' she told him huskily, desperately wrenching her attention away and trying to focus it on something else.

She could feel the heat invading her stomach, and knew with sick certainty that he must be as aware of the pointed thrust of her nipples against the fabric of her blouse as she was herself.

He neither spoke nor moved, and she couldn't bring herself to look directly at him, rushing into hasty speech in an effort to pretend that she was behaving perfectly normally.

'I was reading your manuscript. It's ... it's wonderful,' she told him honestly. 'Kit and Bellengaria are so real ... especially Bellengaria. I really felt I could identify with her.'

She barely knew what she was saying, driven by an urgent need to fill the silence between them with something, even if that something was only words...a frail and very fragile barrier to keep them apart, to stop her from closing the distance between them and reaching out to touch him as she ached to do. But least they *were* a barrier.

And then Oliver destroyed it by saying thickly, 'Bellengaria *is* you. I didn't want her to be...I didn't plan for her to be. She was only to be a very minor character...a symbol of all the women who are too vain and too selfish to risk themselves in any way for anyone. I had planned for her to abort Kit's child and in doing so kill herself, but she wouldn't let me mould her the way I wanted to. She kept refusing to let me twist her personality into the shape I wanted. She kept on insisting on being someone I didn't want her to be, on making me feel things I didn't want to feel,' he told her rawly. And then he said with a groan, 'Oh, God, don't look at me like that.'

As he reached for her, she stepped forward and into his arms, raising her face for his kiss, any voice of caution that might have counselled her drowned out by the furious thud of her heart and the rush

of pleasure through her veins, sucking her down
into its dangerous undertow.

He didn't kiss her the way he had done in his
dream, and although physically she missed the raw
sensuality of that embrace, emotionally she delighted in his tender hesitancy as his lips feathered
against hers, giving her time to withdraw from him
if she chose to do so.

When she didn't, the pressure of his mouth
deepened, his tongue-tip tracing the trembling contours of her lips, exploring them avidly with barely
restrained hunger. She felt the control he was ex-
ercising over himself in the hard bite of his fingers
against her arms and the smothered sound he made
against her mouth as he tensed and then withdrew
from her slightly.

'I lied to you yesterday,' he told her huskily. 'And
I lied to myself. God help me, I think I'm half-way
to falling in love with you already.'

'Me, or Bellengaria?' Francesca asked him unsteadily, trying to keep her head, trying not to let
the fierce stab of delight his admission brought sway
her into headlong folly.

'She is you,' he told her drily.

'And you had intended her to be your Kristie,
hadn't you?' Francesca questioned intuitively.

Oliver paused and she held her breath, wondering whether he would be able to be honest with
her, or if the habit of holding her sex at arm's length
was now too deeply ingrained to be overset. She
had sensed, in reading his book, Kit's resentment
at his feelings for Bellengaria, and she suspected
that Oliver was equally resentful of his own feelings
for her.

'I did initially subconsciously model Bellengaria on her...or rather on her type of woman,' he agreed at last. 'It was a way of expiating my own guilt and bitterness over Katie's death. If I'd had less pride...if I'd fought to keep her, she would have been alive today.'

Francesca put her hand on his, silently conveying her sympathy and understanding, knowing that there was nothing she could say to him that had not already been said.

After a moment he said thickly to her, 'There must be at least a hundred thousand reasons why you and I aren't right for one another, but right now all I can think of is how good you feel in my arms.' As they closed round her, he added unsteadily, 'Do you remember me telling you that some day there was going to be a man who was going to look at you and want to possess all the secrets of your heart and soul, and that nothing was going to stand in his way?'

'Yes,' Francesca whispered shakily.

He was caressing her arms, his fingers smoothing her flesh with growing impatience.

'I want to take you to my bed and make love to you, Francesca... I want to see your eyes cloud with desire for me. I want to hear you cry out with pleasure and need when I touch you. I want...'

'Show me...show me what you want, Oliver,' she interrupted him in a breathless, eager voice she barely recognised as her own, and she clung to him as he lifted her off her feet and pushed open his bedroom door.

For all her inexperience, she felt no fear or hesitation as he undressed her, only a quivering awareness of how the light, delicate touch of his fingers made her feel, and the pleasure it promised.

He studied her body when he had removed the last of her clothing, and Francesca held her breath, suddenly wondering painfully if he was comparing her to the other women he had known, and then the thought was gone as she saw the hard burn of colour in his face and the hot glitter of desire that turned the silver-ice eyes to molten mercury. His hands moved over her with slow deliberation.

'I've wanted you like this from the first moment I saw you,' he muttered thickly, gathering her against his own body so that her flesh took heat from his and then burned in the delicious friction of his flesh against her own.

His hands spanned her hips, making her stomach quiver, the tiny, fluttering waves of sensation increasing frantically when he bent his head and kissed the soft swell of her belly.

Without knowing what she was doing, her nails dug sharply into his shoulders, soft shudders pulsing through her. She ached for the freedom to show him her love, not just in the passive acceptance of his caresses, but in reciprocating them.

His hands traced the contours of her body, shaping the narrowness of her waist, smoothing over her ribcage to gentle the aching tension in her breasts. His mouth moved softly on the tender flesh of her throat, his tongue teasing the wild pulse that beat frantically in it, his exploration of her flesh slow and thorough so that by the time he reached her mouth she was wild for the taste and heat of it, welcoming the fierce thrust of his tongue with soft cries of pleasure, arching her body into the aroused heat of his with quickening rhythmic movements that mirrored the heated thrust of his tongue in the soft sweetness of her mouth, until he stilled the frantic urgency of her unlessoned body and lifted himself slightly away from her, rasping thickly into her throat, 'Slowly, my love, slowly!' And then, as he drew a shuddering, steadying breath, he took her hands and placed them against his chest so that she could feel the wild race of his heart, and then bent his head to feather his mouth lightly against her own as he tried to temper the fierce urgency of their mutual need.

But it was too late for temperance, and beneath the gentling touch of his mouth Francesca's clung and burned as she fought to match his greater control and lost, her muted cry of need shattering his self-control like too thinly blown glass.

He taught her things about both herself and him she had never dreamed could happen, and she was his willing pupil, tormenting his body with hot, open-mouthed kisses which she scattered recklessly across his throat and chest until he groaned out loud and then subjected her to the same torture, punishing the quivering tips of her breasts with the delicate lash of his tongue until she was driven to seek relief by capturing his head and curling her fingers into his hair, holding him imprisoned against her flesh until he made amends for his torment by suckling the swollen, tormented peaks of flesh into throbbing fires of ecstasy.

It was then that he took her hands and placed them on his own arousal, and, after the first shock of intimacy, the knowledge that he was as vulnerable to this all-encompassing drive for possession as she herself was allowed her to listen to the instincts which whispered to her how best to pleasure him.

When he entered her he did so tenderly and carefully, but she was eagerly ready for him, dismissing the small stab of pain without hesitation, enticing him to move deep within her and holding him there until his body shuddered and he gasped her name in urgent need, flooding her with the physical release of his desire for her at the same time as the tiny shudders of sensation coiling through her erupted into shattering explosions of pleasure.

Afterwards she lay, limp and dazed, only partly able to comprehend what had happened. She felt almost as though her body had dissociated itself from her mind, and that the two were entirely separate entities.

Gradually she came back down to earth and opened eyelids that felt as though they were weighted down and heavy, to look uncertainly at Oliver.

'Is it...is it always like that?' she asked him shyly, and then watched tensely as dark colour burned his face and his eyes turned from ice to liquid heat and he told her thickly, 'Not for me. For me, it's never been like that.'

And then he took her in his arms and held her so tightly she could hardly breathe, his head buried in the warm hollow of her neck. She felt the convulsive moment of his throat, and when he raised his head she saw that his lashes were clinging together in short, damp clusters, and a huge surge of love for him overwhelmed her, locking her throat as she witnessed the evidence of his emotion.

'Oh, God, Francesca,' he moaned, and she was unaware of the cause of his distress until he took her hand and placed it on his aroused flesh.

'See what you do to me,' he muttered, his hands trembling against her face as he cupped it and caressed her mouth with his own.

At his low, urgent moan her own flesh took fire, and she drew him down against her.

There was no work done that day. They slept through the afternoon entwined together in Oliver's bed, and then later she showered and dressed while he cooked them a meal.

They ate in front of the sitting-room fire, where later Oliver made love to her again. She fell asleep in his arms and awoke in them the following morning.

They were in his bed. He had carried her there while she slept, and she stretched and yawned and leaned down to caress the smooth, firm flesh of his shoulder, first with her lips and then with her teeth until he woke up and took hold of her.

'I'll have to get dressed. We need food,' she told him softly.

'And I need to work,' Oliver agreed reluctantly.

They had made no plans for the future, but Francesca was confident that they would share it, just as she was confident that although, unlike her, he had not said so in as many words, Oliver cared for her.

She had not been able to hold back from the heady pleasure of whispering to him how she felt, and she smiled a secret woman's smile to herself as she dressed, remembering how those soft, betraying words had driven him to possess her with fierce passion.

It was a clean, cold morning with a washed-out, pale blue sky and a sharp yellow sun. Faint, ethereal eddies of mist lingered in the hollows of the garden, soft veils of secret mystery that added a touch of haunting strangeness to the familiar landscape. Cold and clear, with a hint of frost in the air, the weather tempted her to walk to the village instead of taking Beatrice's car.

She was half-way down the drive when the telephone started to ring, and Oliver was in the shower, so that neither of them heard it, and because she had chosen to walk to the village instead of drive she missed seeing the hired Ford that turned off the main road and into the private lane that led only to Oliver's cottage.

The man driving it had the smooth olive complexion of the Southern European. He was plump and small of stature, with thinning black hair and snapping dark eyes like black olives.

He was Francesca's uncle by marriage, and he had been sent to England by her grandfather, ostensibly on business, but in reality to discover just why it was that his granddaughter had requested her parents to send her her text-books and why, when they were questioned about her whereabouts, they had refused to give him any clear answers.

A letter from Francesca to her parents had given him her address, and now her uncle, like the dutiful son-in-law he was, was determined to fulfil his mission and ensure that nothing would upset the Duca's plans for his granddaughter's future. Plans which, as yet, neither Francesca nor her parents knew anything about.

Marco puffed out his chest slightly with pride. He felt privileged that *il Duca* had confided in him, and he would do everything in his power to ensure that his father-in-law was not disappointed in him.

He and his wife had no children of his own, and he neither understood nor approved of Francesca. She had too much of her English mother in her; the girl who had infected the Duca's only son with her radical and uncomfortable English ideas.

In the privacy of their own suite of rooms, he had confided to his wife his belief that it was this Englishness in Francesca which had led to Paolo's marrying someone else and so casting shame on the entire di Valeria family, and she had agreed.

CHAPTER TEN

At the same moment that Marco was getting out of his hired car and knocking on Oliver's front door, Francesca was laughing at the antics of some ducks chasing a piece of bread, which a previous passer-by had thrown to them.

She had never experienced such exhilaration before...such intense joy, that one moment she was close to tears, the next to laughter. Such highs and lows were alien to her, and yet just to think of Oliver brought her such a rush of joy that her emotions almost threatened to choke her.

Oliver invited his unexpected guest into the sitting-room.

'So, you say my niece has gone to the village,' Marco was saying. 'A pity that I have missed her, but no doubt I shall catch up with her when she returns to the home of Mr and Mrs Chalmers. I understand that she has been staying here with you during their absence.'

It had come as a shock to make that discovery; that Francesca could have so far forgotten her di Valeria upbringing as to stay at the house of an unmarried man unchaperoned, and now that Marco had seen that man, all his worst fears were confirmed. He dared not think what *il Duca*'s response would be to the information he would have to carry back to him. Carlo knew that *il Duca* was negotiating another marriage for Francesca. Not even her parents knew of these negotiations. Only he had been trusted with *il Duca*'s confidences.

He had seen the wary caution narrow Oliver's eyes as he introduced himself, and now he made full use of the power *il Duca* had given him to say importantly, 'It is her grandfather's wish that Francesca returns home with all speed. He wishes to announce her betrothal at Christmas and the wedding will take place shortly afterwards.' He pursed his lips and added, 'I understand that Francesca has been working for you. Her grandfather will not like that. How long will Francesca be, do you suppose?'

'I have no idea,' Oliver told him curtly, his face hard with tension and anger. 'But I would prefer you to discuss whatever it is you have to say to her somewhere else. She will be returning to the Chalmers' home this morning. I suggest you make contact with her there.' He paused and then demanded grimly, 'I take it that Francesca knew when she left Italy that her grandfather would be making these arrangements for her future.'

Marco didn't hesitate.

'But of course,' he agreed innocently. 'How could she not do? *Il Duca* is not a monster, *signor*. He would not take such an important step without consulting Francesca as to her wishes. She is a naughty girl not to have told you of these plans, but then, girls like to play tricks of this kind on our sex, don't they?' he commented, inviting Oliver to join him in his male acceptance of such feminine foibles.

'They do, indeed,' Oliver agreed grimly. 'And now, if you wouldn't mind leaving, I have work to do.'

Francesca heard the clatter of the typewriter as she walked into the cottage. It sounded harsh and angry, and her muscles tensed reflectively before she chided herself for her folly, and her too vivid imagination.

And yet, as she paused outside the closed study door, a curl of nervousness tightened through her lower stomach.

What was there to feel nervous about? she asked herself firmly as she turned the handle and tried to ignore the growing feeling of disquiet invading her.

Of course, she hadn't expected Oliver to greet her on the doorstep with open arms and cries of delight that she had returned, but he must surely have heard her come in; he must know that she was bound to be experiencing a very natural hesitancy and uncertainty brought on both by their physical distance—virtually the first time they had been apart in twenty-four hours—and the opportunity during her walk to think rationally about the commitment she had made to him. He was far too intuitive not to do so.

As she opened the door and walked into the room, she saw that he was sitting behind his desk. He didn't lift his head or acknowledge her presence in any way at all.

'Oliver,' she said uncertainly, her apprehension growing swiftly and chillingly.

He lifted his head and looked at her, and the shock of that cold, contemptuous glance made her gasp.

'I'd like you to pack your things and leave,' he announced unemotionally, the silver-ice eyes burning her with freezing rejection.

'Oliver!' she protested huskily.

He didn't answer her, and one tiny corner of her mind worked itself free of shock and saw that the hand that lay on his desk was clenched into a hard, angry fist. She swallowed her pride and shock and asked him quietly, 'What's wrong?'

'Nothing's wrong,' he told her coldly. 'I simply want you to leave. That *is* my prerogative, I believe, since this *is* my house!'

Her feelings showed clearly in her eyes. She heard him make a harsh sound that could have been contempt or distress. Either way, it seemed not to matter. Hot tears burned her eyes. She couldn't believe what was happening.

'You can't mean this,' she protested despairingly. 'After last night...'

'Last night never happened,' he told her harshly. 'I have nothing to say to you, Francesca. Nothing. Now please leave.'

She had the feeling that if she refused he would eject her forcibly. Her mind couldn't take in what was happening and, like an automaton, she went upstairs and put her things into her case with hands that shook.

Her books were in Oliver's study, but she knew that she wouldn't go and get them. She couldn't face that cold stare a second time. Reaction was beginning to set in, and as she walked downstairs she started to shake.

She made it to Beatrice's car without collapsing, but half-way back to the Chalmers' house she had to pull the car into the side of the road so that she could be sick. Cold and trembling with shock and disbelief, she got back into the car and drove it slowly the remaining distance back.

Elliott saw her arrive from his study. He watched her get out of the car, and then frowned as he witnessed the slowness of her movements.

'Beatrice,' he called to his wife, who was standing on the opposite side of the room, talking to Henrietta. 'Francesca's back. I think you'd better go out to her...'

'Why, what's wrong?' Beatrice demanded hurrying over to join him, her shocked, 'Oh, my God, what's happened to her?' echoing her husband's concern.

Francesca was barely aware of Beatrice coming out to put her arm round her and guide her into the house. She was shivering visibly now, her teeth chattering, her hands icy cold, betraying all the symptoms of someone deep in shock, although she herself didn't know it.

Beatrice and Henrietta put her to bed, but it was only Beatrice who witnessed the slow slide of tears down her face as she turned her face to the wall and said painfully, 'He sent me away... I thought it was real. I thought there was something special, but it was all self-delusion.' And then she started to shiver again while Beatrice stood helplessly at her side and mentally cursed Oliver Newton for whatever it was he had done to reduce her to this state.

It was Henrietta who grimly produced a sleeping tablet and volunteered to sit with Francesca until it took effect.

'I think we ought to telephone Oliver,' Beatrice told Elliott.

'Why?' Elliott asked her grimly. 'I warned you that this might happen,' he reminded her, his expression softening a little as he saw her face. 'I'm sorry... That was uncalled for, but I'm as concerned about her as you are. Did that uncle of hers say where he was staying this morning when he called to see her?'

Beatrice shook her head.

'No. I was in such a fluster, what with just having arrived home and the children hungry...that and the discovery that Francesca wasn't here, that once I'd found her note and realised what had happened, and passed that information on to her uncle together with Oliver's address, I completely forgot to ask where Francesca could get in touch with him. Oh, Elliott...what on earth do you think happened?'

The look he gave her made her lower her eyes and bite her bottom lip.

'You think...you think he actually seduced her and then...threw her out?' she asked him dismay. 'Oh, Elliott...no...'

'I don't know about seduced,' Elliott told her grimly, ignoring her soft protest to tell her calmly, 'Whatever else Oliver might be guilty of, Bea, I doubt that it's rape...'

'But don't you think we ought to find out what happened? I mean we're virtually standing *in loco parentis* to Francesca.'

Elliott's eyebrows rose. 'A woman of twenty-four? I doubt that Francesca herself would welcome our interference. No, I'm afraid it's as I said to you from the first... I did warn you,' he added for a second time.

'Oh, poor Francesca... Oh, Elliott, I feel so guilty!' Beatrice cried.

'You're too tender-hearted,' Elliott told her, not for the first time, trying to distract her by adding. 'Wasn't that a letter I saw from Miranda?'

'Yes, she's hoping to make it home for Christmas, but she'll have to get back to Edinburgh almost immediately after Boxing Day. Apparently she's volunteered to help with the costumes for a charity pantomime that's being put on to raise money for a local hospital. William should be home as well.'

'And Lucilla and Nick, by the sound of it,' Elliott reminded her. 'At least, that's what she said in New York.'

'Mmm. You know, I think Lucilla might be pregnant,' Beatrice told him, momentarily distracted. 'She didn't say anything, but she had a special look about her... a softness...'

Elliott's eyebrows rose.

'You think so? I thought she didn't want any children...'

'There was a time when she didn't want a husband,' Beatrice reminded him wryly, but talking about husbands and babies reminded her of Francesca, and she worried at her bottom lip and wondered anxiously what she could do to help the girl lying asleep upstairs.

For Francesca reality had taken on a hazy, un-focused image that blurred whenever she tried to reach out and touch it. Although, after the first shock of waking up and realising what had happened, she managed to conceal her distress from the people around her. Or at least she thought she had managed it until she walked into Beatrice's sitting-room three days after her return from Oliver's house and realised from the silence that greeted her that Beatrice and Elliott had been talking about her.

Beatrice looked both worried and guilty and, watching her, Francesca suddenly knew that she couldn't stay here any more.

Oliver's rejection of her wasn't some fictitious dream from which she was going to wake up to find herself held safely in his arms. *That* had been the dream. This hard, cold pain inside her... *this* was reality.

She announced her intentions as calmly as though her return had been planned for days and not seconds, and after a first betraying gasp of shock Beatrice rallied and said lightly, 'Oh, will you be going back with your uncle, then?'

'My uncle?'

Francesca stared at her.

'Yes. He called here the morning we got back, asking for you... apparently he was in England on business. He asked where you were and I told him you were staying with Oliver. I gave him Oliver's address... Didn't he come round to see you?'

'No . . . no, he didn't,' Francesca told her slowly. 'What was he like, my uncle?'

Beatrice described him swiftly.

'Ah, yes . . . Marco. He is married to my father's eldest sister. Odd that he should have business over here. As far as I know, my grandfather has no business connections at all in this country. Marco works for my grandfather,' she explained quietly, 'in the family business.'

And she knew with instant and clear insight that Oliver's rejection of her was somehow bound up with her uncle.

Hope . . . a hope that had been extinguished completely as the days went by and Oliver made no attempt to get in touch with her, sprang up inside her. She would go and see him . . . ask him to explain, to tell her what it was her uncle had said to him to turn him against her; why he had made him change so dramatically towards her.

She excused herself on the pretext that she had letters to post. Beatrice and Elliott watched her go.

'Do you think she's going to see him?' Beatrice asked her husband.

'If she is, she's making a mistake,' Elliott told her grimly.

'But why? How can you *say* that, when we don't know . . .'

'I know,' Elliott told her hardily. 'I didn't tell you, but I bumped into Oliver in the village yesterday. He refused to mention Francesca's name at all. He told me he was leaving the area for an unknown length of time, and the way he said it made it more than clear that the very last thing he intended to discuss with anyone was the reason for his departure. He left late last night.'

'Oh, poor Francesca,' Beatrice protested. 'Did you see her face, Elliott? It was as though someone had switched on a light inside her...'

Elliott let her weep against his shoulder as he smoothed her dark hair and reflected on the folly of mankind.

The cottage was shut up... empty. Francesca realised that immediately, and then she knew that there was to be no going back... that Oliver had made his decision and intended to stand by it.

She flew home two days later. Her parents, who met her at the airport, were shocked by her appearance, and even more shocked when she told them that she didn't want to return to the *palazzo*.

'I need to talk to you both,' she told them, adding bitterly, 'somewhere private.'

She told them everything, sparing herself nothing, even when she heard her father's indrawn breath of shock when she announced that she and Oliver had been lovers.

Painfully she went on to tell them how he had rejected her. 'It had something to do with Uncle Marco... I know it. What was he doing in England?'

'I don't know,' her father admitted. 'I knew he was away on business, but I had no idea he had gone to England. Do you want me to talk to your grandfather?'

Francesca looked squarely at him, and in her face he saw a shadow of his father's implacable will.

'No,' she said quietly. '*I* will do it.'

Her grandfather had a suite of rooms on the second floor of the *palazzo*, furnished with antiques and art treasures. These rooms were sacrosanct, and no member of the family entered them without prior invitation... or at least no member of the family *had* done so, until Francesca walked in on him unannounced the morning after her return home.

She was staying in a hotel, stubbornly refusing to return home, and the instant she walked into his study, she saw beyond her grandfather's swiftly concealed shock a gloating satisfaction that was quickly masked as he said urbanely, 'Francesca, *cara*. How good it is to have you home... even if you do seem to have forgotten your manners while you have been away. However, it is no matter... Come and sit down and talk to me. Tell me how you liked England.'

'I have a better idea...' Francesca said evenly. 'Why don't *you* tell *me* instead what Uncle Marco was doing in England?'

'Marco was in England?' her grandfather commented after the briefest pause. 'I did not know.'

'You're lying, *Nonno*,' Francesca said swiftly, and saw the urbanity give way to biting anger as he stood up and said furiously,

'You dare to say that to me, you who have come closer to bringing the di Valeria name to shame than any other member of this family...'

'I haven't come here to talk about Paolo,' Francesca interrupted him tersely.

'Then who have you come to talk about? The man who turned you from his bed and his home the moment he had had all he wanted of you?' he sneered contemptuously. 'It is just as well that you have come home, Francesca. With any luck you will be married before anyone can discover how much you have disgraced us.'

'Married?' Francesca questioned him sharply, wild hope leaping in her breast.

He gave her his most Machiavellian smile and said with deliberate cruelty, 'Not to Mr Oliver Newton, I'm afraid, if that's what you are hoping. He does not want you, Francesca. No, the marriage I am talking of is to Guido Marchanti. I have approached his family. They are agreeable to the marriage. You...'

'Guido Marchanti?' Francesca cut in ruthlessly. 'Are you mad? He is five years younger than me and a self-confessed drug addict. If you think I am going to marry him...if you think I am going to marry *anyone*...'

'But, my dear, you allowed this...this... Englishman to take you to his bed. In a few months' time you could well be glad of a wedding ring and a husband...'

'Never,' Francesca told him passionately, once she had digested his taunting comment. 'I am free of you now, *Nonno*,' she told him abruptly. 'I am not your willing pawn any longer...'

'While you live under this roof you will obey my will,' *il Duca* stormed back at her, forgetting in his fury at her stubbornness that the days were gone when parents and guardians could oblige their offspring to marry as they wished, forgetting everything but his fierce determination that this recalcitrant granddaughter of his should do as he bid. 'You are *my* grandchild,' he thundered, but it was too late. Francesca had already left.

Her father caught her as she came flying down the stairs. He took one look at her flushed face and too bright eyes and said quietly, *'Cara...'*

'It's too late, Father... I cannot stay here any more. Do you know what grandfather had planned for me?'

He listened in silence when she told him, his expression growing steadily more bitter.

'So *that* is why he sent Marco to England,' he said at last. 'That man has always enjoyed playing his stooge. For the sake of your brothers and their inheritance, your mother and I cannot leave this place, you know that, but *you* are my daughter, Francesca, and I will not let you be forced into such a situation. Let me write to this man... this Oliver...'

Francesca shook her head. 'No. It would do no good. I can't stay here though, Father. I will find somewhere else to live.'

'I shall do that for you,' her father told her firmly, and when she insisted fiercely that she wanted nothing that came to her tainted by her grandfather's wealth, her father shook his head and said softly, 'When we came back here your mother begged me not to sell the villa I bought her when we were first married. I paid for that villa with money I earned myself when I was not working for your grandfather. Stay there, Francesca, and promise me that you will not do anything foolish. Your mother and I will visit you as often as we can.'

He looked so drawn and concerned that Francesca found herself reassuring him that he was not to worry about her, and that she would be happy to live in the small house which had once before been her home.

Christmas came and went, and she did not know whether to be glad or sorry when she discovered she had not conceived Oliver's child.

The New Year arrived and the streets of Venice were filled with masqueraders. Francesca buried herself in her work. It was her sole panacea. She had found a job working for an ancient *marchese* who wanted to write a history of his family.

She learned from her mother that her grandfather had announced that, as far as the family was concerned, she no longer existed.

'He still thinks you will weaken and come back,' her mother told her on one of her weekly visits.

'To marry at his bidding? Never!'

In England January brought a heavy fall of snow to the Cotswolds; it also brought Oliver home from his stay in Hollywood, where he had been discussing his now completed book with his agent.

His agent loved it, although he had tried desperately to get Oliver to change the ending.

'To have the woman . . . Bellengaria—odd name, that—killed? It just doesn't make sense. Not when the guy loves her and she loves him . . .'

And he thought he heard Oliver say in response to him, 'It was the only way I could get rid of her.'

Three days after his return, he called on Beatrice and Elliott and found them on the verge of leaving for Italy.

'It's the wedding,' Beatrice explained uncomfortably to him, both surprised and confused by his visit. She resented his assumption that he was

welcome in their home after what he had done to
Francesca, but because she was a gentle woman she
couldn't find the words to make her feelings plain.

'So... her uncle was right, then,' Oliver said bitterly. 'She was an excellent actress, I'll give her that.
Do convey my congratulations to the bride, won't
you?' he added harshly, while Beatrice stared at him
in bewilderment.

It was Elliott who came to her rescue, taking hold
of her arm and holding it warningly as he said
calmly, 'I think you must have got your wires
crossed somewhere, Oliver. It isn't Francesca who's
getting married, but the brother of an old friend
of ours.'

Beneath his warning grip, Beatrice tensed and he
said quietly to her, 'Isn't that our daughter I can
hear crying?'

'But she's...' Fast asleep, Beatrice had been about
to say, but she caught his warning look just in time
and said in a flustered voice, 'Oh, yes... of course.
I'd better go up to her.'

Half an hour later she saw Oliver's car drive away
in a flurry of gravel, the tyres spinning urgently.

'Where's Oliver off to in such a hurry?' she demanded in bewilderment when she found Elliott
watching him.

'Italy, I suspect,' Elliott told her. 'What time did
you say our flight was? I've got a couple of phone
calls to make...'

'Elliott Chalmers!' she warned him direfully. 'I
want to know exactly what's going on.'

*   *   *

Venice was damp and Francesca felt permanently chilled to the bone. She never seemed able to get properly warm, but it wasn't until her mother commented in distress about how thin she had become that she looked at herself properly and realised how her love for Oliver had changed her.

The days seemed to blur into a constant ache of misery from which there was no escape.

Hurrying homeward one wet evening, having worked late, she came to an abrupt halt outside her front door, as she glimpsed the shadow of a man lingering there. As she hesitated, he turned round and stepped from the shadows.

'Oliver!'

The shock held her motionless.

She blinked the rain from her eyelashes, unable to believe what she was seeing. So now she was hallucinating as well as everything else, she thought bitterly, ignoring the figure coming towards her.

He caught hold of her as she drew level with him, the bite of his fingers telling her that he was real!

'I need to talk to you,' he said quietly.

A dozen acid retorts rose to her lips, but none of them were uttered.

'How did you find me?' she asked huskily instead.

'Your father gave me your address.'

'Just like that?' She was unable to conceal her shock, or the tremble of bitterness in her voice.

'I believe I was threatening to dismember your grandfather at the time,' Oliver elucidated grimly. 'I've missed you,' he added rawly. 'Oh, God, Francesca, how I've missed you.'

She swayed towards him yearningly, and then stopped herself.

'I know everything...' Oliver told her softly. 'I know all about how your grandfather sent your uncle to England to find out what you were doing and to make sure you came home to marry Guido Marchanti.'

'You sent me away,' Francesca told him, deep in the memory of her pain.

'Because I thought you were just using me...lying to me... Oh, God, we can't discuss this out here.'

It was true. They were already attracting a good deal of interest. She opened her bag and searched tensely for her key, so nervous that when she eventually found it she almost dropped it, and then couldn't steady her hand enough to put it into the lock.

Oliver took it from her and she saw that his hand trembled almost as much as her own.

'Perhaps if we were to try together...' he suggested huskily, and the warmth of his hand over the cold thinness of her own brought a hot surge of tears to her eyes to blind her and leave her weak.

They were inside before she realised it, the door slamming closed beneath Oliver's weight, his arms going round her, locking fiercely so that she couldn't escape. His voice murmured words of love she had never thought to hear, his mouth tasting her tears, brushing in anguish against her eyes as he closed them, and then silencing her protests as he kissed her until she couldn't control herself any longer and she fell apart in his arms, giving way to shocked pain as she relived his rejection of her.

For what felt like a lifetime she drowned in the pleasure of his touch... his need, and then, with a soft sob, she tore herself out of his arms.

'Oliver, it's no good,' she told him painfully. 'You say you've missed me... that you love and want me, but I can't forget...'

'How much I've hurt you,' he finished for her.

He had suffered, too. She could see that, and she ached to reassure him, but she was frightened of giving her trust a second time and having it thrown back in her face. 'I don't blame you,' he told her soberly, and then added huskily, 'Francesca, can we sit down? I could only get a seat on a flight to Rome, and then I had to stand most of the way on a train... bearing in mind the state of my emotions at the time...'

No wonder he looked exhausted, Francesca thought with a pang of love.

'Of course.' She led him into her sitting-room. She had done nothing to the place since her arrival. Feeling as she had, her surroundings were of little interest to her and, although the house was reasonably comfortable, it did not have the shabby warmth of Oliver's cottage. She realised, though, when he spoke, that she had mistaken the reason for his frowning inspection of her home.

'Do you know, there were many times at the cottage when I would look up and see your head bent over your work, and I would remind myself of how different your real surroundings must be... the granddaughter of a very wealthy man... brought up in luxury. I did it to warn myself against falling in love with you.'

'Luxuries aren't everything,' Francesca told him shakily, emotion clogging her throat at the memories he was stirring.

'Not to you, maybe,' Oliver agreed wryly, 'but for me the knowledge that financially a very wide gulf indeed existed between us was just another level in the barrier of my defences against loving you. Another weight to the already exhausting burden of my insecurities, if you prefer.'

'I can understand how what happened with Kristie would leave you feeling that no woman could be trusted,' Francesca agreed huskily, immediately understanding him. 'I can see that you would want to protect yourself against that kind of hurt again...but after we had made love...after you knew... I thought then that we had made a commitment to one another...that...' Her lips started to tremble and she couldn't go on.

'Oh, God, Francesca, don't,' Oliver begged her, racked by guilt and remorse. 'I should have known...should have trusted you. Perhaps in some way I was even subconsciously looking for a way to distance myself from you. It was too much too soon: the struggle with the book and the realisation that Bellengaria wouldn't be pushed into the role I wanted for her...the knowledge that *you* could not be pushed into the role I wanted for you...safely on the outskirts of my life. The cataclysm of our lovemaking, and then, the first moment I had alone to think, your uncle arrived.'

'What exactly did he tell you?' Francesca asked him quietly. Pride had restrained her from demanding an explanation from Marco himself, but

she had a pretty fair idea of what must have
happened.

'He expressed concern that I had perhaps been
deceived by you. He explained that your grandfather was concerned about you. He gave me to
understand that there was an agreement between
you and your grandfather that he would be ar-
ranging a marriage for you!'

'And you believed him?' Francesca asked sadly.

'Yes. Yes...' he confirmed harshly and then,
seeing her face, added, 'Oh, God, Francesca, what
have I done to you? To both of us? I'd better leave.
I shouldn't have come here, but these last weeks
have shown me how impossible it is to live without
you. When I heard that you weren't getting
married...when Elliott told me...all I could think
of was how quickly I could be with you... that and
what I was going to do to your grandfather...'

'That's why I'm living here,' Francesca told him.
'I couldn't stay at the *palazzo*. Not after what he'd
done.'

'No. Your father explained everything to me. I
think at first he had the same murderous intentions
towards *me* as I had towards your grandfather, but
once I told him I loved you...'

'You told him *that*?'

'How else do you think I managed to get this
address from him?' Oliver asked her grimly.
'Francesca, I wouldn't blame you if you sent me
away... but show me the mercy of doing it quickly,
because, believe me, I think I've reached the end
of my endurance.'

Send him away... As he said the words, she knew
she couldn't do it. And, with that knowledge, the

pain, the hurt, the anguish of his rejection melted away.

She went to him and knelt at his side, placing her hands on his shoulders so that she could draw him down to her.

'How can I, when I love you so much?' she asked him softly.

She caught her breath in her throat at the look he gave her. He made a sound against her hair, his arms going round her to hold almost too tightly. Instinctively she rocked him soothingly, as though he were a child, feeling his body shudder with the force of his emotion.

For a long time they remained like that, neither of them speaking, and then Oliver released her and said shakily, 'I think I'd better find myself a hotel for the night.'

'You can stay here,' Francesca offered huskily, but to her surprise he shook his head.

'No...' He saw her face and took hold of her again. 'Not because I don't *want* to be with you, my love, but for your sake, if nothing else, I think we shall have to observe the conventions until we're married.'

'Married?' She stared at him.

'You do want to marry me, don't you?' he asked her unsteadily.

'Yes,' she told him shakily.

They were married in Venice less than a month later. Her grandfather had insisted on a large formal wedding breakfast, being held at the *palazzo*, which was masterminded by Francesca's aunt and which drove everyone involved in its organisation to the brink of insanity, but, as her father counselled her when she would have insisted on marrying Oliver quietly with only her parents and brothers present, it was her grandfather's way of tacitly acknowledging that he accepted the marriage.

'I don't care if he doesn't accept it,' Francesca had retorted stubbornly. 'After what he's tried to do...'

'He's an old man, *cara*, and stubbornly proud. He thought he was doing what was best for you.'

'Best for the family, don't you mean?' Francesca corrected him drily, but when Oliver added the weight of his arguments to her father's she could no longer resist.

They were going to live in England in the cottage; their children would grow up there. On the morning of their marriage Oliver presented her with a copy of his new book. She turned to the last few pages and read them quickly, a teasing smile curving her mouth.

'So your agent had his way...you changed the ending.'

'I had to,' Oliver told her. 'I could hardly have poor Kit suffering the loss of his love when I had mine, could I, my love?'

Coming Next Month

#1215   FRIEND OR FOE   Jenny Arden
Kira's late husband had given Glenn Mason guardianship over her stepdaughter, Heather—a fact Kira deeply resents. But his responsibility certainly doesn't give Glenn any right to interfere in her life—and sparks fly when he tries!

#1216   LOVERS TOUCH   Penny Jordan
The only way Eleanor de Tressail can keep her promise to her grandfather to keep the estate in the family is a marriage of convenience to wealthy Joss Wycliffe. Only, for Eleanor, it is a case of love.

#1217   NOT WITHOUT LOVE   Roberta Leigh
Julia's assignment is a challenge—to guard an engineer-inventor who has received death threats. Since Rees Denton refuses to have a bodyguard, Julia has to operate undercover as his personal assistant. But how can she watch over him at night?

#1218   WILD JUSTICE   Joanna Mansell
Cassandra has enough problems coping with her overly possessive father, so she is furious when Jared Sinclair lures her to his isolated Scottish home for reasons entirely different from those he's given her. Surely it can't be just for revenge?

#1219   CHERISH THE FLAME   Sandra Marton
Everyone's happy about Paige's forthcoming marriage to Alan Fowler—except his older brother, Quinn, who returns on the eve of the wedding. He tells Paige her father has been embezzling money from the Fowlers for years—and shocks her with the price for his silence!

#1220   THE DEVIL'S SHADOW   Sally Wentworth
Her glamorous sister, Verity, spoiled Charlotte's early romance with Craig Bishop. Now, six years later, with Charlotte's dreams about to come true, Verity seems ready to do it again!

#1221   THE GATHERING DARKNESS   Patricia Wilson
Nurse Julia Redford agrees to accompany her young patient Justine to her guardian's home in the Camargue. Julia has managed to cope with arrogant, overbearing Luc Marchal on her home ground, but once in France, Justine seems fine—and it's Luc who gives Julia problems!

#1222   BRAZILIAN FIRE   Karen van der Zee
Chantal finds the sudden switch of life-styles from small-town America to the glamorous sophistication of Rio more than bewildering. She is even more puzzled by the cool, arrogant Enrico Chamberlain, who seems to hold her in such contempt!

Available in November wherever paperback books are sold, or through Harlequin Reader Service:

In the U.S.
901 Fuhrmann Blvd.
P.O. Box 1397
Buffalo, N.Y. 14240-1397

In Canada
P.O. Box 603
Fort Erie, Ontario
L2A 5X3

Especially for you, Christmas from HARLEQUIN HISTORICALS

An enchanting collection of three Christmas stories by some of your favorite authors captures the spirit of the season in the 1800s

TUMBLEWEED CHRISTMAS by Kristin James

A "Bah, humbug" Texas rancher meets his match in his new housekeeper, a woman determined to bring the spirit of a Tumbleweed Christmas into his life—and love into his heart.

A CINDERELLA CHRISTMAS by Lucy Elliot

The perfect granddaughter, sister and aunt, Mary Hillyer seemed destined for spinsterhood until Jack Gates arrived to discover a woman with dreams and passions that were meant to be shared during a Cinderella Christmas.

HOME FOR CHRISTMAS
by Heather Graham Pozzessere

The magic of the season brings peace Home For Christmas when a Yankee captain and a Southern heiress fall in love during the Civil War.

Look for HARLEQUIN HISTORICALS CHRISTMAS STORIES in November wherever Harlequin books are sold.

HIST-XMAS-1

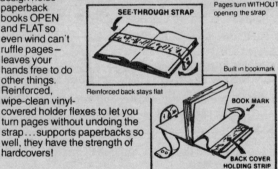